The Bronc Rider Takes a Fall

The Bronc Rider
Takes a Fall

A Tremaynes of Texas Romance

Debra Holt

TULE
PUBLISHING

For My Readers….

We made it to 2021! It seemed to take a long time to arrive, but it is here and I wish nothing but the best for each of you in this new year. This summer, Tule Publishing will be launching my latest series, The Tremaynes of Texas. I am very excited about this newest series of mine. And this book, **The Bronc Rider Takes a Fall**, is the third in the series of four books.

Here is a little secret for you as you are about to read this book. The entire time I was writing the character of my hero… Trey Tremayne… I was picturing only one person in the role as I was writing and I think most of you might know the character. If you are as big a fan of Yellowstone, the television series, as I am, then you are familiar with the son… Casey. And for whatever reason, when I began writing Trey Tremayne, that television character was right there in the back of my brain. Of course, I polished him up a little bit and made him into a rodeo Romeo with the ladies. But his looks and thoughtful, introspective manner with those he cares for… I think you'll recognize and help you envision the hero as you read his story.

And I want to give a shout out to the wonderful ladies in marketing and artwork at Tule… Nikki, Cyndi, and Lee and her team… they are super to work with and so helpful. And I can't wait to hear what you think of the cover artwork in this series… they always bring my brand (Texas bluebonnets) to the covers in beautiful authenticity. And as you read this latest series, be assured I am hard at work on another one… or two… series! Let's make 2021 a year we all want to remember.

Happy Reading!
Debra

Chapter One

"WHO NEEDS A man? I can do this just fine. Just a little more this way maybe—and..." The shriek came next as the stepladder wobbled. There was a creaking sound, and the stepladder went backward while Laurie Wilkes went forward, her hands grabbing handfuls of empty air as she tried to stop her freefall. The ivy planter she was in the process of trying to balance on the shelf above her head was launched sideways from its precarious perch.

Trey Tremayne moved quickly from his stance in the doorway of the general store. His arms shot out on reflex to break the woman's fall, but his foot encountered the moisture from the overturned ivy at the same time. He did manage to grab the woman around the waist just before he ended up on his backside, his body effectively breaking her fall on the hard wooden flooring. The air went out of his lungs and stars shot across eyelids squeezed shut as sudden shafts of pain shot throughout his body, particularly where his head met the immovable floor. The old ticking clock on the wall counted the beats of silence that followed all the commotion.

"Oh no! I'm so very…" Laurie began her apology once the shock had worn off enough, trying not to inflict more damage than she already had on the prone male beneath her. She planted her palms on either side of the man's head, attempting to leverage herself up a bit. Eyes widened in horror as she noted the unmistakable familiar prone figure. "Oh no, help, someone—help!" She screamed out the last words while she tried to scramble up, but two strong hands at her waist locked her in place.

"Lady, I'm not dead…*yet*." The deep voice halted her movements in a heartbeat. "Although, I may have some serious damage below the belt if you don't watch what your knee is doing right now. And no need to scream the place down."

"Thank heavens, you're okay." Laurie breathed in relief just before her eyes widened with some unknown emotion. Then he saw a crimson stain put color in the fair skin of her cheeks as comprehension dawned on her at his words. She immediately stilled as if she were on a tightrope and too afraid to move in either direction. He'd laugh at the whole scenario if his head wasn't hurting and his already injured side wasn't in a slow burn.

"I'll raise you up, and you can get to your knees—*carefully*—and then push up from there. Count of three."

It worked and she was on her feet in a flash. "Here, let me help." She stepped forward, her hand outstretched.

Seriously? For a moment, Trey considered ignoring it.

But his ingrained manners got the best of him. His large palm swallowed hers, and she added her other hand on top and put great effort in helping him off the floor. For a petite female, she did have some power in that grip. Once on his feet, he noted she came just to his shoulder. He liked his women taller… and blond…hair long, well-endowed body. It was hard to gauge her hair as it was platted into one long braid and wound around the crown of her head and fastened. It was the color of cinnamon with maybe some streaks of lighter color visible on her forehead. The loose shirt she wore did little to attract attention from the opposite sex. Although when she had landed on him, and he could breathe again, his hands had registered some nice curves on the periphery of his pain.

Brown-eyed females were normally his favorite but her eyes were a deep blue-green color with some tiny gold flecks…most odd, but in an appealing sort of way. Trey also knew false lashes when he saw them. Hers were definitely the real thing. A dusting of light freckles lay on the bridge of her pert nose. And there was an interesting petite indentation on her chin about the perfect size for a thumb to rest.

His gaze next landed on the graceful, bow-shaped mouth with its slightly fuller bottom lip—which she seemed to have a nervous habit of nipping with her teeth, as she was doing at the moment. A sudden urge shot through him to see if it was as soft as it looked. *Hold on.* Had he hit his head harder than he thought? Because that sort of thinking came with a huge

"Danger" sign flashing in his brain. He was on a medical sabbatical and that included from women, too.

"Are you okay? I'm sorry I fell on you. That ladder…"

"Should be thrown out," he interjected. "It's old and obviously unstable. What made you climb it? You should have known better."

Those eyes blinked a couple of times and then slowly narrowed on him. Her hands returned to her sides—something which he was more aware of than he cared to admit.

"My grandfather has used it just fine for years. I didn't see any harm in continuing its use. As I said, I am…"

"Are you serious?!" His eyes weren't on her; they were glued to the floor.

Her gaze followed his. Hands flew to her face, and she took a quick couple of steps backward, the sudden intake of her breath loud enough for anyone to hear. The cowboy slowly bent and retrieved the cream Stetson from the floor where she had just been standing directly on its crown…damp soil from the planter being ground in quite well by her sneakers.

His ability to hold his temper was something Trey was quite proud of as he had matured over the years. However, he was hanging on the edge of maintaining that record just in the space of a handful of minutes since coming upon the female in front of him—frozen in wide-eyed horror at the battered and no longer pristine hat he held in his hands.

"I'm so very sorry…*again*. Can it be fixed? I'll replace it."

"It was brand-new. It was also a gift from my sister."

"I would say the 's' word again if it would do any good, but it seems I just keep repeating it." Her voice trailed off. "Was there something I could help you with? You were coming into the store for some reason."

He was? Trey had to get his mind back from the various places it had gone in just the last few minutes. Few things generally rattled him, but she had managed to go from zero to seventy in that department in nothing flat. Who was she anyway? What was there about her that seemed vaguely familiar? Dare he even want to know?

"Worms. I remember how the storekeeper here had the best and freshest. I'll speak to him if he's around."

"That would be my grandfather. He's not available. I'm running the store while he's out for a few weeks in Florida. I can help you with those worms. They're out back." She moved toward the doorway in the corner, looking back expectantly for him to follow.

"I can come back later."

She stopped and faced him, hands going to slim hips. "Either you want to catch some big fish, or you don't. Those worms seem to do the trick." She didn't get to add anything else, as a little form appeared at the top of the stairs behind the counter.

"Are you going fishing, mister? My gramps told me there are some mighty big fish in the Red Sandy."

Trey nodded at the red-headed little boy. "That's my plan."

The boy came down the steps two at a time. "My gramps showed me some of the best places to go after the biggest ones. Want me to show you?"

The woman's hands landed on his little shoulders and pulled him back to stand at her side. "Hold on, T.J. Remember you were brought up with some manners."

He glanced at her and then returned his green-eyed gaze to the tall man. He stuck out his hand. "Sorry. I'm T.J. Monroe. Pleased to meet you."

Trey could feel a smile tugging at the corners of his mouth, but he held it in check. Seriousness was called for. He took hold of the little boy's hand and was surprised at how much firmness the boy put into it. Someone had been teaching him well. "Nice to meet you, T.J. I'm Trey Tremayne. Good grip you have there. Your dad teach you that?"

"No, sir. He died. But my mom says you can tell a lot about someone by their handshake. A strong handshake and eye contact makes a good imer...impers..."

"Impression," she finished for the child.

Well stick my foot into my mouth. He could kick himself for assuming and then mentioning the kid's dad. Yet, his response had been matter-of-fact...not one to seek any sympathy. The woman must be his mother? That would explain the absence of any ring on her hand...a widow. And why he had noted that earlier was another reason to kick himself. He didn't need any female interfering with his hiatus from the arena.

"That's very true. How old are you?"

"I'm seven, but I'll be eight in two weeks. Wow, you're a real live cowboy? I saw your picture on the rodeo poster my gramps has in his office. Do you ride bulls? Do you get thrown off a lot?"

"T.J.! That is not very polite."

Trey shook his head and tried to make light of the moment. He should be used to the question. "I try my best to *not* get tossed off, and I ride bucking broncs...not bulls."

The boy fell silent and a shadow crossed over the freckled face. Trey's antennae went up a notch or two. "Broncs buck a lot higher and faster than those slow, fat bulls."

"I was about to show Mr. Tremayne where the worms are kept," the woman interceded. "Why don't you lead the way?"

"Sure." That brought the smile back. "We've got some really fat ones."

A few minutes later, with T.J.'s help, a container of some of the biggest, blackest worms Trey had ever seen were on the counter. He handed over his payment with a glance at the little boy. "Thanks for the help in selecting these. They just might do the trick."

"Anytime." The child took a couple of steps on the stairs. "I hope you have fun fishing. Maybe you'll catch Old

Sourpuss."

"Old Sourpuss?"

"My gramps calls him that. He says he's the biggest old fish he ever saw, but no one ever catches him. He saw him once, and his face reminded him of someone who eats a really sour pickle. That's why he named him that."

Trey had to chuckle in spite of himself. "Well, that would be an interesting fish to see." A thought came to him, and he held back for a moment. He couldn't believe he was seriously considering it. He took another covert look at the small, freckle-faced boy still taking his time—now on the fourth step. He was a sucker for kids. And without a dad and his grandfather apparently gone for a while…he probably didn't get to go fishing much of late.

"Say, T.J.…. If it's okay with your mom, maybe you could show me where to find Old Sourpuss?"

The boy's face lit up like a house on fire. "Mom, can I? I'll be careful. I'll do whatever the cowboy says, and I'll even eat the broccoli tonight. Please? Can I go?"

Trey looked at the woman who wore an equally surprised expression at the invitation. He shouldn't have put her on the spot. Although, she had in fact ruined his favorite hat. And she could have maimed his manhood for life when he broke her fall. She sort of owed him. He caught her glance. He looked down at the hat lying on the countertop for a couple of moments. Then he glanced up at her. Her eyes narrowed a bit as she read the message loud and clear.

"I realize that I'm basically a stranger and all, but you can check me out with at least half of the other storekeepers in this town. They'll tell you I am harmless and responsible. Plus, if you don't mind sitting and watching people fish for a couple of hours, you are certainly welcome to come along."

Something caused her gaze to darken, and perhaps he felt a slight chill in the air? Had he said something wrong? But then she looked up at him and maybe he had just imagined it?

"When is this fishing expedition to take place?"

"This afternoon, about four."

She turned toward the boy. "Then you better get your chores done."

"Whoopee! I'm going fishing! Thanks, Mom!" He was at the top of the stairs before he remembered something else. He turned and threw a wave at the man. "Thanks a heap, Mr. Tremayne. I'll be ready!" Then he was gone in a flash.

"Nice job," she said, turning back to face Trey. "That bit about your hat... Not above a little extortion?"

"Well, you see it isn't exactly extortion. I just figured you might want to repay me for the hat you ruined and the back you almost broke, and not to mention the blow to my manhood."

There went that soft blush to her cheeks again. For a woman who had a child and thus, had obviously been around a man before, she certainly had the aura of a female unused to male sexual flirting. What was he doing flirting with her anyway? *She wasn't his type.*

"I get the point, Mr. Tremayne. Although I don't know if you know what you just let yourself in for. T.J. has never been fishing in his life. Gramps was meaning to teach him this summer, but then he had his surgery and can't do it. I'm afraid if you thought you were going to have a quiet time of it, you might be in for a surprise. But if you change your mind, I'm sure I can…"

"I won't change my mind, Mrs…? In all this, I guess you and I haven't been properly introduced. You already know my name." He held out his hand.

She looked at it for a second or two. Then she placed her small hand in his. *Nice, smooth skin.* He closed his palm around it, finding the sensation not unpleasant. It was a nice fit.

"Laurie…Laurie Wilkes. I was married for less than a week, so the *Mrs.* just never felt right."

The information brought more questions to mind, such as why would she have a last name different than her son? But they were really none of his business. He was off the mystery sleuth clock for the next month. And Laurie Wilkes might have assaulted him with an ivy plant and old ladder, but he was willing to let bygones be bygones.

"Nice to meet you, Laurie Wilkes. You stay away from that ladder. I might not be around to cushion your fall next time."

"Thanks for the advice. I'm glad I didn't cause you any

long-term damage."

"I think everything is still in working condition."

There went those cheeks again. He picked up his hat and his sack of worms and made his getaway while he could. He had the strangest feeling that his own cheeks were flushed for some odd reason. He hoped he wasn't coming down with something.

Chapter Two

"HE ISN'T COMING." The child's voice came out on a deep sigh. It was a little shaky on the last word. The boy sank down on the couch, leaving his post at the window, his chin landing in his palm as his elbow balanced on his knee. He kept his eyes on the floor in front of him.

Laurie wasn't fooled. She knew he didn't want her to see the telltale sign of a tear or two in those big green eyes. Surely, he wasn't the type of man to make a promise to a child and then purposely let him down without a word otherwise. But then, what did she really know about him? He was some big rodeo star now and still quite the ladies' man according to local gossip she had heard now and then. And she knew his family were very respected ranchers in the area, going back generations. The gossip had also included the fact he was on some sort of vacation or something. Neither was any real guarantee that he would show up.

Of course, there was also the minor fact that he had been the object of her first "real" crush a few thousand years ago. When she had landed on top of the man and looked into those eyes, she had been transported back to her first year of high school. She had been the new kid on the block, so to speak, and was naturally shy and quiet and preferred to stay in the background with her books.

That hadn't stopped her though from joining the long line of females lusting after the "hot jock" on campus, two years ahead of her, who owned the halls he walked with a sexy swagger and a wicked grin that starred in her teen dreams every night. She had worshipped him from afar, knowing she had never come close to being a blip on his radar screen filled with all those "popular" girls. She had to admit it stung even now, knowing he hadn't had a clue, a glimmer of realization of who she was when they faced each other as their adult selves. On the other hand, it had been embarrassing enough with her clumsiness and ruining his hat, so it was just as well she didn't have to be put through him trying to remember the little mouse of a girl she had been. The past could stay the past.

Bottom line, Laurie had to deal with a little boy's disappointment. She had plenty of experience in that department. She glanced at the clock. The man was only nine minutes late. She could buy a little more time. Maybe he had a flat tire. And his cell phone was low on battery power. *Nice try.* Excuses were just that to a little boy counting on catching his first fish.

"You know," she said, folding the last towel in the laundry basket and placing it on the shelf. "Guys aren't the only ones who know how to fish. Gramps took me fishing with him when I was on summer vacation from school. I bet you and I could do just fine. How about it?"

That perked him up enough to get his attention on her and off the floor. "*Really?* We could go now?"

Not exactly how she had planned to spend the next couple of hours. They closed early on Sunday afternoons. She saw the rest of the laundry still waiting to go into the washing machine and the meal that still had to be prepared for dinner. But then she saw the hopefulness in his eyes. Laurie nodded her head. "Sure. I'll grab the fishing rods from the storeroom, and you can go out back and choose some good worms for us." *Worms.* How was she ever going to be able to put one on a hook? Gramps always did that for her. *One step at a time.*

T.J. picked out the dozen best worms he could find and scooped them into the container. He grabbed one of his gramps's old fishing caps from the rack next to the back door and scrambled down the stairs into the store in record time. Laurie had changed into a pair of jeans that she would sacrifice to getting up close and personal with a smelly fish or two. She found one of her grandfather's cotton shirts, a couple sizes too big for her, and slipped it on over her blue tank top. She rolled the long sleeves to above her elbows. Shoving her feet into the pair of well-broken-in sneakers, she then grabbed a floppy brimmed sun hat off the nearby shelf. She wasn't going to a fashion show by any means. And on a quiet Sunday afternoon in McKenna Springs, she doubted anyone would be around to take note of her ensemble.

"Are we going now?" T.J. stood with his hand on the doorknob, impatience about to bubble over.

As much as she might have liked, there wasn't anything to do but turn off the lights and lock the door behind them. *Get it over with.* She threw the boy a smile as she held the door for him to exit first. "I'm sure Old Sourpuss will still be waiting when we get there." She turned the key in the lock and slipped it inside her pocket.

"You came!" T.J.'s excited voice brought her attention around quickly to find the tall figure of Trey Tremayne standing at the bottom of the steps leading to the store's wide porch. It was obvious he had changed also—a more serviceable pair of faded denim jeans and the navy T-shirt he wore highlighted what she already had a hint of before—his chest was solid and shoulders broad. The boy she had crushed over had certainly transformed into quite a man. Laurie quickly drew her concentration to the straw cowboy hat he had on his head. It was a safer area.

"I had a bit of a problem with getting the water heater situated since no one's been in the cabin for a while. It took a little longer than I thought. You didn't think I'd stood you up, did you?" His gaze fell on the boy.

"Mom said you were probably busy or something. I knew you'd come cause you're a cowboy and they're good guys and good guys keep their promises."

A hand reached out and ruffled the boy's red head, and

then the gaze moved up to where she still stood. "Busy? Guess you could say that." She had the distinct feeling that he knew that she thought he was not going to show. Under the scrutiny of his gaze, she became aware of his eyes. On first glance, most people would say they were a shade of blue. Under closer inspection, they would see they were really the color of deep aquamarine. They were unusual, faintly hypnotic in their intense regard, and she would wager they saw way too much if one didn't keep their guard up against them.

They had been the first thing that had drawn her to him back in their school days. Those eyes with the long dark lashes and the deep grooves beside his mouth that became evident whenever he grinned had been the stuff her school-girl crush had been born upon. His hair was brownish blond and worn longer than most of the ranchers in the area. But then he was a heartthrob on the rodeo circuit, so he was allowed the popular "scruffy" look…she guessed. It all added up to one dangerous grown-up version of her sexy teen dreamboat. *Geez.*

"I see you have some worms there." Trey turned his attention back to the child.

"My mom was going to take me fishing."

"Really?" This time his eyes returned to hers, and there was a slight lift of the corner of his mouth. Or was it more of a smirk? Did he think she couldn't do it? He was probably one of those macho types who believed fishing was only a *man's* arena. She felt her hackles rise. Her chin rose, and she returned his look dead-on.

"Well, daylight's wasting so we better be on our way." He met the boy's grin with his own.

T.J. looked up at her. "Mom can come with us, too, right?"

"Of course she can. That is if she isn't afraid we'll catch more fish than she will." Both sets of male eyes were trained on her. *He thinks I'll wimp out.*

"As you said, we're wasting daylight."

WHERE HAD HIS "vacation" taken a wrong turn? That would be the moment he had to come to the rescue of a certain female. Then he had volunteered to take a child fishing. Now, he was sweating in the heat on a riverbank when he had planned to be in an air-conditioned cabin, probably watching a sports show through closed eyelids. If he were a smart man, that's what he *should* be doing. *So much for being smart.*

There was another irritant buzzing around inside his brain. He couldn't shake the feeling there was something about the woman that he couldn't quite put his finger on. Had their paths crossed before? He didn't think so, but still...it was odd. Trey's eyes moved along the bank to where Laurie Wilkes was watching the fishing line of her rod as it disappeared into the almost clear depths. *Surely, he'd remember her.*

With the dark lenses of his aviator glasses shielding his eyes, he was able to cut his eyes away from the cork bobbing on the end of his line to cast a few glances in her direction as she bent to reply to something her son said as he reached into the carton for another big worm. *Very nice.* Not the worm, but the nicely shaped bottom in the snug jeans. Maybe there was something to be said for things that came in petite packages after all. Just about then, she straightened, shrugging out of the men's large-size cotton shirt…using the long sleeves to tie it securely around her waist. *Oh boy.* The afternoon temp had to be gaining. That petite figure had some very nice curves to it. He shifted his stance, very little thought on the cork being pulled under the water.

"Hey! You've got a fish! Aren't you going to bring him in?" The little boy's excitement snapped his attention back to the matter at hand. Trey flipped the lock on the reel and began to bring whatever was on the end of his hook in to shore.

"T.J., you stand here beside me and when I tell you, you can place the net under him for me, okay?" He instructed the boy on what to do while he was intent on not losing whatever it was that fought him on the other end of the line. The boy stood ready with the small net held in both hands, his concentration much the same as that of a major-league catcher about to make a huge play. "Stand easy, he's almost in sight."

"I see him! Is that Old Sourpuss?"

"I doubt it," Trey replied, sorry he had to douse the child's hopes. "This is probably one of his grandkids, by the feel of his weight on the line." The catfish was a nice size. He did his best to get off the hook, swishing his tail as he cleared the water. "Bring the net up under him... Good job. Hold it steady while I release the hook." Trey grabbed the squirming catch under his gills and worked the hook loose. He placed the fish inside the net and watched as the boy carefully moved it to rest over the bucket. Trey bent and helped him with the release of the fish. "Good job. That makes two caught so far."

"Wish I could catch one." So far, T.J.'s hook had come up empty. The disappointment clouded the youngster's eyes.

"You will. Fishing is a sport of patience. You get your hook baited and out there again. I'm going to sit a spell on this tree stump, and it will be up to you and your mom to catch the rest of the fish." Trey leaned his rod and reel against the trunk of the cypress tree behind him and proceeded to settle onto the old stump at its base. He took his hat off for a moment and wiped his forehead free of sweat. A little Texas heat never bothered him before, but then he wasn't back a hundred percent either from receiving a couple of good swift jabs to his side from the hooves of Red Dog, the bronc that unseated him in short work out of the chute in Montana.

"Mom, I need this worm on my line." The boy held up another fat specimen and held it out to the woman who stood a couple of feet away. Trey had to give her credit. He had an idea that touching the worms was the very last thing she wanted to do. He could step forward and help her out. *Or not.* Of course, if he didn't and she did something silly like stick a hook in her finger, then he would feel like a loser. *Not happening.*

"I think your mom needs a new worm on her hook, too," he said, stepping up next to Laurie. "Why don't you hold on to the rods while I bait both hooks?" He didn't wait for her reply but handed the fishing gear to her. The hooks were ready to go back in the water in no time at all. "Okay, why don't you try this area right here, T.J., and we'll have your mom give it a try beside that big tree."

Laurie's eyes flew to his. "I wouldn't want to interfere in the streak you're on. You *have* caught all the fish so far."

"That's why it's time for me to take a rest and let you both catch up. Be my guest," he replied along with a grin. "Do you want me to help you get your line set in the water?"

"No, thank you." There was no hesitation in her reply. The glint in those deep blue-green eyes was a message all its own. "I think I can handle that."

Trey had to admit she handled that just fine. He settled on the ground, leaning back against the base of the tree. He pushed his hat a little farther down on his forehead, the dark lenses going back on his eyes. Situated as he was, he could keep an eye on both the boy and his mom. Although, it might be wise for him to not spend too much time watching the shapely woman in the form-fitting tank top.

His gaze was too prone to find its way to the interesting shadow of cleavage that the navy material highlighted in its dip along the neckline. Just then she turned her head and her gaze narrowed on him. He experienced a quick stab of guilt. If he didn't know better, he might think she could read his mind, even with the lenses giving his eyes cover. As quickly as she locked on him, her expression changed, and her head jerked back to the river.

"Something's on my line!"

"Geez, Mom… Pull it in. Hurry!"

Trey was on his feet in an instant and beside her just as quick. He resisted the urge to grab for the rod and bring the fish in for her. Something told him that she wouldn't appreciate the interference.

"Use the reel nice and slow. Don't jerk it."

"It feels big. Oh, no… I think it's stuck on something!"

"It might have gone under the ledge of a rock beneath the surface. Let me see what I can do." He reached out for the equipment. At that moment, Laurie gave a jerk, then another one on the rod, and out of the water shot a nice-sized bass, fighting for all its worth on the end of the line that she was quickly reeling in. She swung the rod around and the fish managed to smack Trey up the side of his head, its tail sending the hat on his head flying off and into the water. The sudden move caused the surprised man to jump back, a hand trying to make a saving grab for his hat. That's when his feet slid on the slippery mud of the bank, and he was in the water with a large splash.

Laurie froze in place, the fish lost its fight for a second, and no one spoke a word for a few long moments. Not even T.J. ventured a comment from where he stood with his mouth agape. The whole scene might have been comical…to someone else. None of the three of them were laughing.

Trey managed to get his feet under him on the slippery limestone bottom and stood up, the water level reaching midway on his chest. He wasn't hot any longer; the water was cold and delivered a shock when he first went under. One hand swept the wet hair back over his head and his eyes registered another fact. He hastily looked around and located his hat, being moved along by the current down the river, a couple of feet out from the shoreline.

"T.J.! Leave it alone. Stay where…" Laurie's words were cut off by the sound of another splash. Trey turned in time to see the boy going under the water. Then there was a strangled scream and another body hit the water.

Trey reached the boy first and his arms grabbed him just as his red head bobbed above the water. He lifted him up with an arm around his waist. A split second later, Laurie broke the water and her hands reached for her son. The water was deeper than she was tall, so Trey ended up with T.J. in one arm, and a sputtering, upset female in the other.

"Just settle down," he told both of them. "Everyone is okay. I'll get us to shore if you'll just cooperate and be still." Luckily, both the woman and boy followed his terse instructions. The current was flowing fairly strongly in a couple of spots, and he found his footing having to slow down. Slowly, he managed to reach the shallows and hoisted the boy onto the bank. Next, he swung Laurie up in his arms and took a couple more steps until he let her feet touch the dry bank. She scrambled out of his arms almost as fast as that fish had fought the line he wanted free from. Trey leveraged himself out of the water and joined the pair on the bank. They all resembled drowned rats.

"T.J., you are never to go into any river like that ever—"

"But Mom, I had to get Mr. Tremayne's hat," he spoke up, at the same time his hand shot into the air. "And I did!" For a moment, all eyes were on the sopping wet, no longer cream-colored hat, clasped in his hand held above his head in a show of triumph to match the wide grin on his face.

Trey reached out and took the hat, his gaze resting on it a moment before he slowly locked the dark look on the woman. "Thanks, T.J.," he said. Laurie's eyes fell on the hat in his hand.

"Lady," he began, using all his willpower to exert extreme control over his words, "do you have something against my hats? You've managed to ruin my two best in just the space of one day."

Trey didn't wait for a reply. He turned and stomped

along the riverbank, grabbing the fishing gear as he went, and then headed toward his pickup parked a few yards away. They could follow or not.

"I didn't catch my fish yet. And his rod and reel went into the river and the fish got away." T.J.'s voice was low and barely audible. "Guess he won't take me fishing with him again."

"Let's not mention fishing any more today." Laurie's arm rested around his small shoulders as they walked toward the truck where Trey rummaged inside the silver toolbox across the back, under the rear window. He muttered something and then slammed the top down and put the lock back in place. Opening the front driver's side door, he tossed a rain slicker and an all-weather jacket across the space to where Laurie stood with the passenger door open.

"Use these to sit on. I don't need the seats soaked, too." He bunched up the poncho in his hands and used it to sit on as he slid underneath the steering wheel.

"At least you have leather seats. It won't be so bad that…" Her voice trailed off as she saw the muscles in his jaw clinch a couple of times, his darkened blue eyes pinning her in place. *Not a good conversation starter.* She situated T.J. on the back seat and then took her place in the front. The rest of the trip back to town was made in silence.

Chapter Three

"SO, I HEARD you met Trey Tremayne."

"You could say that." Laurie kept her reply to Mel's observance to a minimum. The less said the better. If she could just forget the last twenty-four hours ever happened, that would be even better.

"I hear, from the chatter over at The Diner on the Square that he's really good-looking…'hot as sin' I think that was the prevailing term used, to be precise." The woman arched a look at Laurie who studied the invoices a bit more closely. "What do you think?"

With a soft sigh, Laurie laid the paperwork down and looked at the woman. Mel Crawford taught history at the local high school and had for almost forty years. In fact, she had taught Laurie when she transferred from Faris to McKenna Springs at the end of her sophomore year. She helped out Gramps on weekends and whenever he needed to be away from the store, and she was off. Plus, she was like the proverbial wise owl that saw everything, heard everything, and spoke her mind *often* on everything. Laurie knew it would be best to face things head-on.

"To be honest, I don't think the man will darken this doorstep any time soon…if *ever*. In fact, I think it's a safe bet that he wants nothing to do with anyone here."

"According to Darcy, he's a very pleasant sort."

"Well, when people say they got off on the right foot with someone…you can say we got off on the *left* one. Just leave it at that." Laurie began placing the latest magazines on the rack and removing the older ones. Hopefully, Mel would get the hint and find something to occupy herself other than the cowboy. That hope was short-lived.

"He's going to be around for a few weeks. He's on some sort of medical leave, according to what I picked up from Florence over at the propane store. And he's friends with the McKenna's and wanted a place to lay low and be quiet…away from their big operations over in Faris."

Laurie knew she had to ask. "And how did you end up finding out that information from Florence?"

"I needed to schedule a delivery for our lake cabin. She happened to mention she had just finished a run out to the McKenna cabin. Seems she met the man, and she agrees with the general assessment that he is one sexy fellow…and *single*."

"I know I will regret asking this, but he just offered up his personal medical information to Florence while she was delivering his propane?"

"No, don't be a silly goose. Her sister-in-law, Mary Waddel, is Doc Simmons's receptionist. Seems the man needed to see the doctor yesterday…something about a fall and some damage to his side. She couldn't give details of course… That *is* private information."

Shaking her head, Laurie was constantly amazed about the ability of news to travel around a town the size of McKenna Springs with the speed it did. The town was small compared to most, with a little over 4,500 in the town's limits, and another 2,500 or so scattered around the county, and didn't account for Faris's population. The news about his side dismayed her. The fact he had seen a doctor about an injury made her feel bad. Would that have been her fault, too? She did land on him fairly hard when she fell. Memories of that fall and certain aspects of how her body had instantly been aware of his in ways she had all but forgotten about, came rushing in and she quickly dumped the old magazines into the box. She turned to head to the dumpster when the front door opened, and she ran smack into the person who stepped across the threshold at that time.

"Oh, I am so…"

"Let me guess, *you're sorry.*"

The hands on her upper arms heated the bare skin and her mind went blank at the sudden appearance of the man who was never going to darken their doorstep again. *So much for wishful thinking.*

Then her mind flashed on the fact that he had an injury, and she had just thrust a cardboard box into his side. *Was* she trying to harm this man? "You took the words right out of my mouth." *So there.* "Hope your side is okay. Need more worms?"

Did she really just say that? Would she ever be able to stop sliding backward to that gauche, silly schoolgirl whenever he came around? She was a grown woman for heaven's sake and one he didn't even remember. Best to keep it that way, too.

A twitch at the side of those well-chiseled lips let her know that there was something he found amusing. *Her?*

"I never said there was anything wrong with my side. Are you a psychic, too?"

"No." Why did he still fluster her thoughts so much? *He's just a man. Just like half the population. No big deal.* "How can we help you today?"

"I was told that packages were usually delivered here. I'm expecting one. I took a chance and took my life in my hands, but I needed to stop by and see if it's arrived."

Laurie heard some shuffling behind the counter, and then Mel got into the mix. "Nothing's been delivered here in the last couple of days. You must be the friend of Davis McKenna that's staying at his cabin for a while?"

Trey moved his attention to the older woman who stood watching with interest the interaction between the man and Laurie. His hands released their hold on Laurie's arms as he nodded at Mel. Stepping forward, he turned a smile on the woman, his hand going out to her over the counter.

"Trey Tremayne. Yes, I'm staying at the place on his ranch for a while. And you haven't changed a bit, Mrs.

Crawford."

Mel returned the smile and handshake, a crease of lines across her forehead as she searched her memory. Then a broad smile broke out on her face. "Well, I'll be! That's right, I did get hired one summer to tutor you as I recall now. You were laid up with a broken leg and arm…and your dad hired me to help keep your studies up. I am surprised you remembered me."

"Yes, ma'am. I had a run in with a rank horse and he won. I remember that you taught me a lot and it was interesting. You earned me an A when I got caught up with my work. It's good to see you again, Mrs. Crawford."

"Call me Mel. We aren't formal around here, and you're all grown up and a real rodeo star now, to boot! I never would have imagined that one."

His laugh was deep and spontaneous. "I know. I did take a few falls back then. But I guess I had to learn the hard way how to stay on the back of a horse." They laughed.

"As I said, everyone grows up…often in the most surprising ways. Isn't that right, Laurie Lou?" Her glance suddenly brought Laurie into the conversation even as she was trying to move quietly toward an escape route. She halted in her tracks when the assessing cobalt gaze swung to land on her. He saved her making a reply.

"Laurie Lou? Why does that name…" He cut the words off himself as it was clear the lightbulb had illuminated the memory she hoped would stay in the dark. "I remember *now. I knew* there was something about you."

"Don't worry about it. Some people are just forgettable." She shot Mel a look before she turned away. "I'm taking these to the storeroom." Mustering as much dignity as she could, she hoped her exit was clear in its finality on the subject. Laurie didn't pause until she reached the storeroom and stepped inside. Then her shoulders went limp and she felt deflated.

Why should it matter so much that he hadn't remembered her on his own? She was being childish. And why did he have to remember her at all? High school was ages ago. And she had grown up a lot. She had been through a lot. And she was a mother. She certainly didn't travel in the same rarified orbit as a rodeo celebrity.

If she thought she had found a safe refuge, she was proved wrong. A shadow fell across the floor in front of her, and she whirled to find the tall cowboy framed in the doorway. If that was a look of pity in his eyes, she would just shrivel and die on the spot! Whatever was behind the look was quickly overshadowed by the slow smile that creased his face and deepened those dimples.

"This is an employee's-only area. Mel can help you out front."

"I promise to not come past the doorway," he countered. *Darn him.* He hadn't lost that ridiculous ability to charm his way past anything or anyone. "I just wanted to set the record straight. I *do* remember the smart girl who got most of us jocks through our English literature class. You worked in the library during lunch hour, and I remember you were also the one winning most of the academic awards at the assemblies. See? You *are* unforgettable. Although I should be upset with you for keeping me in the dark this long."

"It was a long time ago. People tend to forget their school days." *I hope.* "Was there anything else you needed in the store?"

Trey took a couple of steps toward her and then stopped... much too close. She had to look upward a bit...more than a bit. *Why couldn't I have been taller?* She felt at a disadvantage in more ways than one. Being this close, she was able to see that the pupils were flecked with sparks of deeper cobalt blue and could cause a person to be caught staring if they weren't careful. She planned to be careful.

"I just wanted to check on your son. I trust I can be allowed to come into your storeroom for that reason." He wasn't asking, but she was too busy trying to keep the loud sound of her beating heart from being heard to contradict him.

"I hope T.J. is none the worse for his impromptu swim yesterday?" His question caught her by surprise, along with his concern for her son.

"He has a slight earache today. Other than that, there's no lasting harm done. Just a large dose of disappointment at not catching a fish. Nothing he can't get over."

"I hope he gets to feeling better soon. I'm sure Old

Sourpuss will still be there whenever he gets to go back to the river." He paused, seeming to search for something else to say. "How about you? Are you eager to get back to fishing?"

"It's not high on my list of 'must do's.'" She needed to seize the opportunity while she had it. The small talk could wait. "We didn't get a chance to thank you yesterday. I appreciate the time you took with T.J. I'm sorry that your vacation got off to such a start. I just want you to know that you gave a little boy a memory he won't soon forget."

"And you? Will you soon forget it?" Something about the way he said the words made her mouth go dry, and her fingers tightened on the box. *Oh, golly gee—why couldn't she be one of those sophisticated females for just five minutes?*

"I'm not going to forget your kindness. If there's any way I can repay the favor, I hope you'll let me know."

His eyebrows shot up and a blue glitter shown in the eyes still focused on her. His voice lowered, obviously mindful they weren't alone in the store. "Now that lends itself to a whole lot of thoughts on the subject." And Laurie slowly shook her head.

"You're good. That high school macho cuteness has been refined. I imagine that flirty line and smooth innuendo go a long way with your fans at the rodeos…the female ones. And that lets me out. I'm a single working mom who grew up a while ago." Laurie could tell by the smile fading from his face that he hadn't expected her response. She hadn't expected she could deliver it so matter-of-the-factly.

"I see that. And if I overstepped, I apologize. Guess you got me pegged from your vast experience with rodeo cowboys. Relax, little Laurie Lou… You're safe. I've kept you from your work long enough. You take care and stay away from ladders." The wink he gave her was swoon-worthy if ever there was one, but she stood her ground with some silly half smile plastered to her face until he had left her alone.

Slow steps carried her back into the main store area, past the rows of canned goods and the rack of ladies' hosiery. Laurie stopped in front of the barrel of saltwater taffy pieces. Her mind was not on candy. Her gaze went out the wide store window and followed the tall figure across the street, watching him disappear inside the large black double cab pickup.

"My, my," Mel spoke behind her, her voice slicing through the silence like an alarm clock that got Laurie's attention back inside the store. "This is shaping up to be an interesting summer."

Laurie didn't reply. She turned and headed in the direction of the office. Making a fool of herself two days in a row was bad enough. She didn't need to do it in front of an audience.

Chapter Four

"THAT'LL BE TWO meat loaf plates, both with green beans and corn. One iced tea and one large milk for the young man here." Darcy read the order back from her pad, before letting a smile fall on the youngster. The Diner on the Square was very busy for a Thursday evening. Laurie had picked up an unusually quiet T.J. from the scout meeting and decided it might be nice and much easier to stop by the local diner for dinner rather than wrestle with cooking and homework after a long day of inventory. She normally tried to have a home-cooked, well-balanced meal on weeknights for the two of them, but sometimes best laid plans fell to the wayside.

"Correct. I'm glad we got here when we did. Looks like you've got a full house."

"Yes, and Myra called off with a migraine. I had to move Pat into the kitchen to help out Javier with the grill, so I'm running like a chicken with its head cut off. Of course, I may lose a cook too, judging by Javier's face. Pat is an okay waitress, but a real novice in the kitchen."

"I used to spend summers running the poolside grill

while I was in college. I can flip a pretty mean burger, and I have my food handler's permit from the store. I could work the grill for a while if it would help you out. Then Pat could come back out here and waitress."

Darcy hesitated for a moment. It was just about the same time as a loud clang echoed from the kitchen and some colorful language swiftly followed from Javier. Her eyes darted back to Laurie. "I couldn't ask you to do that, after you put in a day at your own business."

"You aren't asking, I'm volunteering." Laurie slid out of the booth. She looked at T.J. "Why don't you sit on the stool at the end of the bar and you can get started on some of your reading homework while I help out Miss Darcy?"

"Sure thing," he said, his eyes lighting up at the prospect of sitting at the bar like the older kids often did.

"I owe you big-time for this, beginning with free dinners tonight."

Laurie didn't know who was more grateful for her arrival, Pat or Javier. She pulled on a red and white checked apron that covered most of her and hastily pulled her hair back with a tie. There was a long line of tickets growing on the wheel in front of her, so she dove in, easily finding the remembered rhythm of working a busy grill. She noticed Javier glanced over a few times, but less and less as the evening progressed. Every now and then, she would take a quick peek out the large serving window to check on T.J. He had his head buried in a book.

About thirty minutes later, Darcy breezed through the doorway and paused at the grill. "You are a lifesaver. If you ever want to quit that general store or maybe take on some extra hours, you have a place right here."

Laurie shot her a grin as she turned over a couple of steaks, their juices sizzling as they hit the hot grill top. She added some freshly cut onions next. "I'll keep that in mind."

"I think T.J. has a quick question for you. I'll watch that order for you if you want to stick your head out there and see."

"Thanks, Darcy. I'll be right back."

Wiping her hands on her apron, she pushed through the swinging door and then came up short. T.J. was seated on the stool where she left him, and he was deep in conversation with the person seated next to him. He caught sight of her at that same moment.

"Hey, Mom! Trey came in to eat, too. Can I eat with him?"

Laurie wished she could just retreat into the kitchen as her eyes locked with those too familiar ones that held an amused glint in them as they made a slow perusal of her. She could just imagine how she looked—the apron was too big for her, and the grill was hot which made her face feel flushed and it had to look the same, not to mention the sticky dampness of her skin from being in a heated kitchen. *Too late now.* She moved to stand at the counter.

"First, I'm sure you need to remember your manners and

36

address him as Mr. Tremayne. And I am sure he would like to eat in peace."

He glanced at the boy and then back to her. "It's good to have some company at the dinner table now and then. And I did give him permission to call me Trey. It sounded too formal the other way, and we're friends. I don't mind it if you don't?" The man looked directly at her, arms folded nonchalantly across his chest as he watched and waited for her next excuse. T.J. used his best "puppy dog" face on her.

"Please, Mom? I won't pester him, I promise."

"Keep that promise." She gave in. It was a relief to escape back to the kitchen. She wished she could figure out how to stop the ridiculous "off-kilter" feeling the man's very appearance exerted over her whenever he was around. She didn't care for the feeling. She was levelheaded and kept her feet planted in reality—until Trey Tremayne had walked back into her life. But since she had punctured what would be his manly pride, she hadn't expected their paths to cross again.

Fifteen minutes later, Annie came through again and flashed a grin. "T.J. is making a good dent in his dinner. And Trey sends his compliments to the chef who grilled his steak. Seems you got it just right."

Laurie tried not to react to the unexpected compliment. Or the sudden information that the woman was on a first-name basis with the man. Just how well did she know him? Laurie quickly shut that thought away. It wasn't any of her business.

"I told Javier to fix your plate now. The rush has died down and we can handle it. So, you can turn in your apron and go be a diner…with my sincerest gratitude. You really saved us tonight."

"To tell the truth," Laurie responded, stepping back and drawing the apron over her head, "it was kind of fun. Took me back to my college days." *Before life took a crazy turn. When life still held a lot of possibilities.* But she didn't voice those last thoughts. Instead, she smiled and tossed the material into the soiled laundry hamper next to the sink.

"I placed your iced tea on the table already." Annie disappeared into the storeroom.

Laurie stepped through the door and saw that T.J. was no longer seated at the bar. Her eyes found him seated at a table in the corner of the diner. Trey sat across from him. They were engaged in a conversation and neither noticed her. She made good her escape into the ladies' room. She needed to try to freshen up a little given the fact she was not going to be able to ignore the other adult at the table. Laurie did the best she could with water and soap, using her fingers to comb through her hair. Her purse held a comb and lip gloss, but it was with her son. When she couldn't put the inevitable off any longer, she squared her shoulders and took a calming breath.

"I'm glad to see you've almost cleaned your plate," Laurie said with a smile for her son as she arrived at the table. In an easy movement, Trey stood and pulled out a chair for her.

"Thank you." She slid into the seat and threw the words and a small smile in the general direction of the man. He returned to his chair without saying a word.

"That's good manners," T.J. observed before spearing the last of the green beans on his plate.

"My mother taught me my manners," Trey replied. "I imagine your mom is good at teaching you some, too."

T.J. nodded his head. "I know how to open the door for old people and ladies. Always say yes, sir and no, sir. Don't talk with food in my mouth…"

"I think he gets the general idea, T.J.," she spoke up. "You should finish all your milk, too." She concentrated on eating her own meal. The sooner she finished, the sooner they could be on their way from the diner.

"You're a lady of many talents," Trey observed, folding his napkin and placing it beside his plate. "I had no idea besides being a store manager, a fishing aficionado, and a very involved mom, you also can grill a steak without reducing it to dry shoe leather. My hat's off to your skills." He flashed a grin at that point. "Or it would be if I had one."

Her fork slipped from her hand to clatter on the edge of her plate. She reclaimed it and met his gaze. "Another example of good manners would be not to bring up embarrassing moments. I can assure you I have not forgotten the demise of both your hats."

"You need to work on your sense of humor. If I can find

humor now in what happened, I think you can, also."

"My sense of humor is just fine."

He looked across at the boy; leaning his arms on the table, he asked him a question. "Is that right, T.J.? Does your mom laugh very much?"

The child gave a quick glance at his mom, seemed to consider something for a moment or two, and then decided. "Not really."

"T.J.! That's not so."

"You laugh a little. Not a whole bunch. Not like some of the other moms do."

"We'll see what we can do about that. In the meantime, I think I have room left for some of the apple pie over there on the counter. What do you think, Mom? Has the young man here earned a slice?"

Her mind had to hurry and switch tracks as Trey was moving things along. "I think since you cleaned your plate, you could have a small slice." She smiled at her son. "Why don't you go over to the bar and ask Miss Darcy very nicely to bring two slices?" He was off like a shot. Her attention swung to nail the man.

"Nice job. You put me on the hot seat with your question, and then used my son to turn up the heat. Yet you stepped in and sent it in another direction. In the future Mr. Tremayne, leave my child out of your game playing." She pushed her chair back and stood, gathering T.J.'s backpack and her purse. "Would you make one slice of that pie to go,

Darcy?" she called across to the woman slicing the pie behind the counter. "Thanks for keeping T.J. company during dinner. Good night." She didn't wait for his response as she moved to join her son at the bar.

"But Mom, why can't we eat with Trey?"

"I've got things to do at home before bed," she responded. "Take your backpack while I get the pie."

Darcy set the to-go container on the bar. "Here you go. Thanks again for everything tonight."

"It was my pleasure. Glad I could do it." She slid the straps of her purse over her shoulder and gave the woman a smile. "If you ever need help again, you know where to call."

"I do indeed. Night, y'all."

Laurie didn't look back when they got to the door, and T.J. turned and gave a wave in the direction of the table where Trey was being served his slice of pie. She was just glad to escape. They had parked around the corner from the diner. She unlocked the door of her compact car, and T.J. scrambled into the passenger seat. She was aware of his disappointment evidenced by the droop at the corners of his mouth as they left the diner and walked to the car. Popping the trunk, she dropped the backpack inside. Before she could close it, a voice behind her startled her and she whirled around.

"You forgot something."

Her hand went to her stomach and she took a couple of deeper breaths to calm the pulse that had raced off the charts. "You startled me! You should make some noise before you sneak up on someone in the dark."

"Excuse me," Trey looked taken aback for a moment, almost apologetic…almost. "I don't think I was sneaking up on you. But I'm sorry if I scared you."

"What did I forget?"

He held up the small white container. "The slice of pie. You left it on the counter."

She reached out and took the pie from him, frustrated with herself for confirming for him what he already must know her to be—a scattered, forgetful, clumsy female. "Thanks." *Awkward silence.* "Well, good…"

"Why do I rub you the wrong way? I've tried to think back over things since you literally fell into my arms off that ladder. Ever since our memorable first meeting, you seem to be walking on hot coals around me…like you'd rather be someplace else. That can definitely be a dent to a guy's ego. And I don't get it. Was there something I did or did not do in high school, or…"

His question was so unexpected and so out of the ordinary, Laurie was speechless. Was this some sort of joke? He certainly looked serious enough. His steady gaze held her immobile.

"I don't think anything I could do or say would dent your ego. And no…this has nothing to do with high school days." The words were out in an instant.

"I can't figure you out. Just when I think I might have an

idea, you skitter off in another direction. I thought us being old friends and all and…"

"Old friends? Being in the same school building doesn't qualify us as being old friends, and I am fairly certain you didn't even know I existed most of the time way back then. And I don't think I'm that hard to understand. I'm grateful for your assistance when I fell. I am also grateful that you took some time to make a little boy happy on a fishing trip. But I also need you to realize that I am just what I said I am. I am a mother with a little boy who can be very impressionable and fasten hero worship easily on someone that may or may not always be the best role model. That's when I have to use some adult judgment."

"I see. So *you* think I'm of questionable character to be around T.J.?" His voice lowered as his gaze met hers. Did she imagine there was a flash of something in those blue depths having nothing so much to do with anger as it might be disappointment? Had her words been harsher than needed? She had been the "momma bear" for so long, perhaps she had become mired down in it? Was the fact that this was Trey Tremayne, the flashy golden boy she remembered from the past, coloring her judgment a bit?

"No, I'm not saying that. It's just hard…hard to accept people at face value sometimes. But you must admit you do have a reputation that precedes you. We don't live in a vacuum here in the country. We get the news about celebrities, especially home-grown ones."

"So I'm guilty of whatever gossip there might be involving me and my being as you put it a 'rodeo cowboy.' I get it. And I hear your warning loud and clear." Trey straightened, and it was like a shade had been drawn over whatever she might see in his gaze now. "You are a good mother, Laurie *Wilkes*. You grew up well. I guess some of us didn't quite make that grade. You both take care and have a good night."

Trey left her standing alone. He said he got her message. So why did she feel like she had just made a huge mistake? Had she been too quick to judge his actions? Had she blown things out of proportion? Why was she second-guessing herself?

"Mom! What's taking so long?" The boy's voice had the effect of a quick reality check. Whatever the reasoning, the outcome was that she doubted hers and Trey Tremayne's paths would cross again. So why didn't that thought make her feel better? Slamming the trunk shut, she hoped she could as easily slam the door on her thoughts involving a certain rodeo cowboy.

Chapter Five

TREY RETURNED TO the cabin in a mood that was not conducive with being on a sabbatical for his health. He went straight to the bedroom, shedding his clothing, kicking off his boots. Then he collapsed on top of the bed, not bothering to turn down the covers, arms folded behind his head and eyes fixed on the slowly turning ceiling fan over his head. He blew out another long, frustrated breath. *Damn woman.*

She was ruining his time away from his work. The time he needed to heal his body and get his mind straight again. If only he hadn't gone into that darn store to buy the worms. Hell, he didn't even like fishing all that much. There was too much sitting still and waiting for something to happen. He preferred movement and action and getting to the nitty-gritty. And yet, here he was, in the middle of nowhere, holding a fishing rod in his hands, and then getting a dressing down…a *scolding*…from a female that was absolutely NOT his type. Any other time, he would simply let it slide into the dust and keep walking away. Why not this time?

The ceiling wasn't giving up any answers to that one. He

was on his own. So, she was an old acquaintance. Except he had an idea that she wasn't one to ever walk down memory lane. Evidently, there had been no good times in high school between them to remember…at least not the kind of "good times" he usually had in those days with members of the opposite sex. That thought frustrated him even more.

Laurie Lou Wilkes wasn't a "fun time to be had" and then move on from sort of girl. One look in those eyes of hers and a man would know that. He had known it. Yet there was something more to it than that. She had triggered something in his brain. And he actually felt a strange disappointment at having been measured by her and coming up short in some fashion. She was only protecting her son…or so she said. From him? Or just any man? Instead of heeding the warning his brain had shot out, he had done just the opposite. He had stuck around. He had even made up a stupid excuse about a package to enter that store one more time. Maybe he was tempting fate. Maybe he was just plain stupid. This enforced medical leave had to be addling his brain. Slowing it down. Making it susceptible to ideas that shouldn't be there in the first place.

She and her son were out of his league. He knew nothing about family dynamics and kids and all of those permanent things. Of course, he had his two nephews and all, and he was their favorite uncle or so they said. He was geared for "temporary" and had managed to keep his personal life on that track. He knew people had labeled him "the lone wolf" and they applied it to both his professional and personal life. He loved women and then he moved on. His publicist had branded him the "Rodeo Romeo" and had spared no energy in putting that in play. There were no strings pulling him back to any one spot. That made it easy for him to concentrate on the next rodeo and the next belt buckle. *Keep the eye on the prize.*

Laurie Wilkes had been made a widow at an early age. Her boy was without a dad. They already had a tough road to walk. They didn't need any transient entanglements in their lives. That's probably why she had reacted to him the way she did after his flirting. She knew better. She was being the "adult" and protecting herself and her child from a situation that had no chance of being anything more. So why should he still be thinking about her? Why did her reaction get inside his head? Or was it *her*...the woman herself...and less about the words? Nothing made it any easier to put it all out of his head.

She had disturbed something within him...something that he had kept compartmentalized and locked away. He didn't need it to gain a toehold in the life he had made. And Laurie Wilkes could do that. She could be a danger; she and her son, both. They represented permanent and Sunday dinners and lawns to mow and colleges to choose. All the things that came with families and giving your heart away to others. Well, he had half a family left, and his heart liked things just the way they were...or had been...until he had come to McKenna Springs and been knocked flat on his back by a woman named Laurie.

"HAVEN'T SEEN YOU in here very much lately. You really must like that cabin of my brother's." Darcy made the comment as she refilled the tea glass in front of the man.

"It's not bad. I suppose it's growing on me."

"And why do I find that such a surprise?" she smiled. Then she answered her own question. "Maybe because I never figured you for a guy to sit still in one place for more than a day if that. You always came through here, and then five minutes later, you were gone. I think the longest you ever stayed put in this town was for Davis's wedding and that was almost two years ago, now."

"Hard to believe it's been that long. Too bad Davis isn't around. Would have been good to catch up with him. Suppose he's past the honeymoon stage and into the old-married-man phase?" He took a swig of his tea and pushed his plate back a bit, resting his arm on the counter in front of him. It was nice to have a bit of conversation with someone besides himself. His self-imposed exile had lasted all of three days. What could hurt coming into town, he told himself earlier, and having a late lunch? The noon crowd would be gone from the diner, and he wouldn't be disturbed. *And less of a chance to bump into a member of the Wilkes family.* That voice in his head needed to take a break, too. He was tired of listening to it of late.

"He's still in the honeymoon phase, but he's about to be in the 'new daddy' phase."

That took Trey by surprise. He shook his head. "Wow. He's going to have a kid. Imagine that."

"*He* isn't going to have it. Stacy is. Just like the woman to still have to do all the work. But he hasn't come down from the clouds yet...and he probably won't for a while. He's been busy building a treehouse...only he hasn't placed it yet, in case he needs to modify the colors and all. They wanted to be surprised, so they won't let the doctor tell them the sex of my nephew or niece. That's why they aren't here right now. They're having one more vacation together without the car seat, stroller, diaper bag, et cetera in tow." She laughed and he grinned. The jangle of the door chimes sounded, and Darcy automatically looked in the newcomer's direction with a welcome.

"Well, howdy, young man. You're right on time. Have a seat and I'll get your order."

A body filled the stool next to him. And then Trey was trapped.

"Hi, Trey! Are you done being busy? Is that why you're back in town? I missed talking to you." The questions came a mile a minute from the little boy, his eyes bright and his grin splitting his face from ear to ear as eagerness bubbled over in his small body.

Knew this was bad idea. Trey was caught. "Yeah, I've been busy. I still am so I was just about to leave." One hand went for the check on the counter in front of him, his other hand for the hat sitting on the other side. Darcy returned with a sack and set it in front of the child.

"You've already got a sack there from the pharmacy. Think you can carry this to-go bag, too? Maybe I could get Joe from the back and he can help you get it to your mom. I'm hoping this soup and ham sandwich will make her feel better. And I added a little something in there for you, too, a slice of that apple pie you like so much. But you can't eat it unless your mom says it's okay. Agreed?"

Trey had halted midway as Darcy's words sunk in. Laurie was ill? He slowly stretched to his full height but did not leave the counter area. *Am I insane?* "So, your mom's not feeling well?"

"She fell. Doctor says she needs to use one of those crunch thingies, but she doesn't like it. She kinda hops around. Mel let me walk down here from the store on my own, but she's standing on the porch watching for me to come back so I have to go but maybe you can come by sometime and…"

"Hold on, there, little man. Take a breath." Darcy grinned.

"Crunch thingies?" Trey asked, his brow furrowing as another suspicion filled his brain. "Do you mean crutches? And did she fall from a ladder by any chance?"

T.J. nodded his head. "Yep, and lots of cans of pickles fell, too. But I picked them up for her and it's okay." He slid off the stool and eyed the larger bag on the counter, before looking to see which pocket might hold the other small sack.

Trey was ahead of him. He handed the money over to Darcy for his meal, and then his fingers took hold of the ends of the white bag. "I'll give you a hand as I need to pick up some things from the store, too." *Liar.* "You lead the way."

"WHAT'S KEEPING T.J.? He shouldn't be this long? Can you still see him?" Laurie called out to the woman standing in front of the large window several feet away from where she was seated on a stool, creating new price tags on the computer screen in front of her.

"He's doing just fine, and I see him. They're on the way back from the diner now." Mel responded with the latest report.

"I know he wants to be a big boy and do..." She stopped mid-sentence. *They're?* "You said they're. Is he with someone? I hope Darcy didn't interrupt her day just to bring my food."

"It's not Darcy." That's all she got from the woman.

Before she could voice her next question, the door opened and T.J. came in, the small bag from the pharmacy held out in front of him, a smile of triumph on his face. "I got your medicine, Mom. And Trey got your food." He turned and glanced back at the tall figure standing just inside the doorway, the man wearing a smug, "I told you so" look in the steady gaze locked on her.

No place to run. And she couldn't run if she had to at the moment. Why had she let T.J. go to the diner? And why wouldn't the floor open up and swallow her right then and there? All valid questions but no answers. She kept her hands on the desk in front of her, but she managed to rise to her feet; her bandaged one was out of view under the desk and she hoped to keep it that way.

Maybe T.J. hadn't shared any information about her accident. But she seriously doubted that to be the case. Trey Tremayne looked like someone who had swallowed the proverbial canary and was ready to enjoy the dessert.

"I'll get to those peaches in the crates in the storeroom now," Mel spoke up. "And T.J., I need some help from you. Let's go." Mel wasn't giving him any time to respond otherwise even though his disappointment shown on his face in having to leave the side of the tall cowboy. She bent to whisper something in his ear as hands on his shoulders guided him from the room. Laurie wished she could go help with peaches, too. But she was stuck.

"Here's your lunch, by the way." Trey moved forward to stand a few feet away from her, his arm reaching toward her, the white bag dangling from his fingers. He waited.

Summoning as much poise as she could, she managed to take one and then two, and then a third step in his direction...with hardly any bobble at all in her gait. And without biting the inside of her cheek when the pain of the movement registered within her. He was not going to see her predicament. She took the bag and set it on the desk behind her, then faced him again, her hands laced in front of the waist of her denim skirt.

"First of all, I was just finishing lunch at the diner when T.J. entered. I was on my way out when I heard the news about your fall. Naturally, I thought I would help out your son with all he had to carry so he wouldn't spill your soup." He stood facing her down, his arms folded over the chest of the chambray shirt he wore. It would have been so much easier for her to respond if she wasn't also aware of the fact of how good he looked and smelled. Those things shouldn't enter into her thinking. *Darn him.*

"And I can imagine who told you. But it isn't anything. Just a little sore and it's practically healed. Thank you for helping T.J. I know you're probably busy." *And now that is your cue to leave.*

"And I hear you fell off a ladder...*again*. I'm betting it's the *same* ladder you shouldn't have been on the first time you fell. Only I wasn't here to break your fall like before. I hear it was jars of pickles or some such?"

He was toying with her for some perverse enjoyment of his. The foot was aching, and her patience was thinning.

"You just came to gloat, so you can leave now. I'm not some sideshow freak for you to ogle at and get your laughs over. You can go be 'Mr. Know-it-all, I'm right' someplace else." She turned, but she did it too fast and a pain shot up her leg and she winced. He saw it.

Hands lifted her in a second and before she could utter a coherent word she had been deposited back on her stool, and the man had gone down on one knee in front of her, his head bent over the foot. Her palms gripped the sides of the stool…not so much in pain, but to keep from the temptation when he removed his hat to reach out and touch the mahogany hair. It was longish on the sides and at the back, with streaks of natural blond highlights that many women would pay big bucks in order to emulate in their own hair. It looked full and soft and…he was just too much to take in when he was touching her foot and ankle in such a way. Concentrate on the here and now and get him out of the store.

"You have it wrapped, and I hear you don't want to fool with crutches. What about a boot?"

"How can I get a boot on it if it's swollen? I manage just fine…unless I have to stand too long or walk too far with an uneven gait. It's okay. And you don't need to stick around any longer. I'm sure you have someplace else to be."

He stood, hands at hips, almost glaring at her. Then he spoke. "You're right. I do have some place to go." Trey Tremayne turned on his booted heel and left her sitting there...*alone.* The door closed behind him. *Finally.* He had got the message, and she could breathe again. His manners needed work. He could have said a civil goodbye. But how civil had she been? That thought zoomed to the forefront of her brain. Not only her foot was hurting but her head was beginning to join in, too. *Food.* She needed to eat her lunch, and all would be better. She might need to work on convincing herself of that one.

STUBBORN WOMAN. SHE could take care of a store. She could be a mother. She could help out friends in need...but she couldn't take care of herself. So why did that matter to him? It shouldn't. *And that is why you went to the pharmacy and now have a walking boot sitting in the seat of your truck...headed back to the store where you are clearly not welcome.*

His brain needed to take a vacation and shut up. Trey didn't need anyone or anything highlighting the fact that he wasn't behaving in his normal way. If he had been wounded in his head and not his side, he might could explain the problem away with a medical reason that made sense. He had stopped taking the painkillers a couple weeks back so that couldn't provide an excuse for him. *No,* this one was on him.

Against all better Trey Tremayne judgment, he was doing the Good Samaritan thing and trying to help out that stubborn woman once again. Would she thank him for it? *NO*…she would probably throw the boot at his head. With that thought, when he parked and got out of the truck in front of the store, he removed his newest hat from his head and left it on the seat of his truck. *Better to be safe than sorry around her.*

Mel was behind the counter when he entered. His gaze did not find the woman he sought.

"She's upstairs. I finally managed to get her up there and get her foot propped up on a pillow on the couch. T.J.'s at scouts, so she's got some quiet time. The door's open." The woman imparted all that information even as she kept her gaze on the paperwork in front of her.

"Thanks. If I don't return soon, best call me some back-up."

"Already planning to do that…or an ambulance." She glanced his way with a knowing look.

He was on the second step when she replied, and he gave her a grin before he continued the climb.

The door was still open, and he paused just inside the threshold. It was a large living room space, with a kitchen that could be seen just off to the left. A sofa and love seat in brown and black plaids was centered in the main room, along with a black leather recliner next to a reading lamp and small table. A television was above the fireplace, its sound muted while the network news played. Large windows looked out over what he assumed to be the street in front of the store. Laurie reclined on the sofa, facing away from him, her head resting on a couch throw pillow and her injured foot on another one.

"Knock, knock." He spoke, announcing his presence from a safe distance.

Immediately, the woman swung her head and moved to situate herself into a sitting position as best she could with her wounded limb. He moved forward into the room until he put himself between the couch and the low wooden table in front of the sofa. He judged it to be sturdy enough, so he took a seat facing her.

"Before you say anything, Mel gave me permission to beard the lioness's den. And just so you know, she's ready to provide backup if needed." He held up his palm to forestall her words. "I know when I had a badly hurt foot once before, actually it was *more* than once, but who's counting…a walking boot really made the difference. It's easy to get on and off with the Velcro straps." He held up the gray boot and gave her a demonstration before she could protest. "You can maneuver up and down stairs easier, provided you go slow and one step at a time. You can even get into an auto. It'll help protect that ankle and foot and give them time to strengthen. I admit it's not the most stylish thing in the world, but you could probably add some bling to it if you really need that sort of thing. And all I ask is that you wait to throw it at me until I at least clear the doorway."

Trey held the boot out toward her…and waited.

Those blue-green eyes had met him with a cold wariness when he had first sat down. They watched him intently while he spoke, the wariness dialing down a bit. Now, they moved from his face to the boot. For a second or two, there was hesitation. Then she reached out and took the cumbersome article from him into both her hands.

"You're right, it's not all that stylish. But I'm not a bling sort of girl, so what does that matter?" The reply didn't expect to garner laughs. She placed the boot on the floor and then swung her legs off the couch. Trey reached over and held the boot's straps open while she fitted her foot inside in slow, careful movements. He could have helped with closing them, but something told him it was best he allowed her. *Baby steps.*

Once it was snug and the closings were secure, she slowly moved to stand. His hand was offered…and tentative fingers reached out to it. He held her hand firm and steady with no move to do more. He was rewarded when a small smile formed on her lips. She raised her head then and looked at him. Her hand was still in his. "It does feel more supportive. And the pain is not there. Thank you for doing this. Seems you rescued me again despite my fall. I appreciate it. You must let me pay you for it."

"Consider it my way of apologizing," he said. "For overstepping the other night and being…well, just let it be part of my apology. I was out of line."

"Thank you. And I'm sorry for being so…for saying such rude things."

"Well, maybe I'm glad you did make note of where I can improve my manners. But let's just let it be forgotten. And I'd like to introduce myself to you. I'm Trey Tremayne and I make no apologies for being a cowboy…by birth and career. But I do know a lady when I am lucky enough to meet one. And you are definitely a lady." They both seemed to realize he still held her hand at the same time. She withdrew hers and he let it go.

"I hadn't expected this. But I thank you for the boot and the apology and for your help. I'm Laurie Wilkes…and I left Laurie Lou behind a while ago, so I thank you for doing the same."

"I will do my best to remember that." He smiled. And she returned it. "So I guess we have a cease fire? Who knows, in ten or twelve years, we might even be friends. I hear a person can't have too many of those."

"Miracles happen every day." They both were locked in an awkward silence but neither seemed inclined to leave it. Then he stepped into the void.

"I've got to be on my way." He remembered one more thing and paused in the doorway, turning to look back at her as she remained by the couch. "And it's time to send that ladder to the junk heap." Then he left her.

The man was infuriating! One moment he was thoughtful; then he was bossy. And she certainly didn't need any man telling her what to do or not. Although she had to admit she was more confused than upset. He had turned into someone that had made her feel cared for with his thoughtfulness. He had been gentle and made sure to not overstep any boundaries…almost to the point of shyness. There was no sign of Trey Tremayne, hot rodeo stud. Well, maybe the hot part was still evident, and she doubted he would ever be able to rid that potency factor from his being, but he was a gentle man…and a gentleman. If that made sense. And he had mentioned friendship. Was that even possible between two such different people? She doubted it. Stranger things had been known to happen. But would it be wise?

Chapter Six

LAURIE WAS FINDING it surprisingly easy three days later to maneuver around with the aid of the walking boot. And her ankle was doing much better when she took off the boot in the evenings and massaged the injured area. Each time she realized that she was healing a little more, she was reminded by her subconscious of the male who took it on himself to get the boot and make sure she wore it. And she knew the time would come when she would have to thank him again…probably when he stopped by to flash an "I told you so" smile her way. She managed to come down the stairs, one step at a time, hand gripping the railing.

Mel grinned at her from behind the counter as she reached the bottom step. "I spoke to your grandfather last night. He called to let me know that he and Faye were done boxing up the last of her house. Tomorrow they would head for Fort Lauderdale and get ready to sail away on that cruise ship honeymoon finally. I didn't mention your latest tango with the ladder. I figured I'd leave that to you. But you look like you're getting around like an old hand at it. You'll be good as new in a few more days."

"I'll be glad of it. This boot is building up my muscles with how heavy it is to lug around all the time. But it doesn't go with the wardrobe." Laurie wore a buttercup-yellow blouse with short sleeves over a white tank top and a white denim skirt that reached to the top of the boot which rose to an inch or so above her knee. A yellow and white headband held her hair back from her face, and it swung free down her back. She chose the outfit because it lifted her spirit with its color on a fresh summer morning.

"I made it just in time," Darcy said, coming through the door of the store. And T.J. was headed down the stairs.

"I saw you from the window upstairs. I have all my stuff in my backpack." He made the final step with a broad smile.

"I'll never be able to repay you for helping out these last few days with running T.J. to scout meetings and such. You are such an angel." Laurie smiled at her friend.

"I enjoy it. It gets me out in the fresh air. I am looking forward to chaperoning this field trip. Besides, that's what friends are for around here. You'd do the same for me if I needed something…like helping out in my kitchen the other night. So let's chalk it up to being good neighbors. Let's get moving T.J."

A quick hug from her son and the pair were out the door, leaving Laurie and Mel behind.

Laurie turned and headed toward the office. "She is such a lifesaver. I haven't tried to drive yet with this boot involved in the process. And… What is this?" Her thoughts were interrupted by the sight of the silver ladder leaning against the side of her office doorway, a big pink bow attached to it.

"Guess you're looking at the new heavy-duty ladder that was dropped off for you early this morning by a certain good-looking cowboy. There isn't a card because he said he was pretty sure you would know the 'admiring friend' who sent it."

Laurie shot the woman a look over her shoulder. "He used the words 'admiring friend' or was that your literary license?"

Mel made the sign of a cross over her chest and raised a palm. "I swear, cross my heart…his words. And by the way, he then went into the storeroom and found the old one. It's in the dumpster out back."

Laurie bit back the words that came to mind. On one hand, he had overstepped…*again*. On the other, he had seen a dangerous situation and took care of it, so that she wouldn't get hurt again. And that made her feel… She didn't know *how* she felt. There wasn't an exact word for it. She should just be gracious and thank him. But she didn't know how to contact him. She had no cell phone number. She knew he was staying at the McKenna lake property, but she wasn't going in search of some cabin in the middle of nowhere. Something told her that he wouldn't stay away for long. Not when there was an opportunity to take credit for the healing of her foot with the boot, and handling of the problem ladder. He was like a bad penny. He'd turn up again.

It was almost midday when the "bad penny" did present himself. Laurie was on the front porch of the general store, rearranging the baskets of fresh purple and red geraniums when the familiar voice caught her off-guard.

"Nice display. I like the colors...especially the yellow."

Laurie swung around to look at the man lounging with one shoulder against a stone pillar a few feet away, his arms crossed over a broad chest, his muscles highlighted by the dark blue material of the T-shirt. The jeans were snug, and his long legs ended in the prerequisite pair of brown leather boots. The heat of the day just went up by twenty degrees. She blinked away any other thoughts that were pressing into her brain about the man. "Yellow? I don't have anything yellow in this display."

"That would be a backward compliment for *you*. You are the yellow part."

And then she felt like a gauche schoolgirl again in his presence. She set the last pot of flowers on the bottom shelf of the display and dusted her hands off. Not that they were particularly dirty or anything, but she needed to release the nervous tension that came on scene with his arrival.

"Thank you for the compliment. And thank you for the new ladder. I would say that I wish you hadn't done that, but I know it would be a waste of time. And I will also say that you were right about the boot. It has made a difference. Thank you...*again*."

"I could just stand here basking in all your thankfulness. But I think the words I will focus on the most...'you were right.' You did just speak those words, correct? I wouldn't want to misquote you when I share them with everyone else."

Laurie's gaze narrowed on Trey. "I was being *nice* and using *good manners* to thank you. Now you are being the arrogant, smart..."

He held up a palm and pushed away from the pillar to step closer. "And let's recall the truce while we can. I was out of line. Thank you for thanking me. You are welcome. Glad I could help. But there is one thing you can do that would be very considerate and show your sincerity in our newfound attempt to be *friends.*"

She fixed him with a look that bordered on a warning, hands on hips, waiting for what he surely wouldn't expect in gratitude. "If you think for one minute that I will..."

"Have lunch with me? You were going to say if I think for one minute that you'll kindly take pity on me and have lunch with me today...then that would be correct. Isn't that what you were meaning to say?"

He had known what she was thinking, and he had stopped her before she could really make a fool of herself and say something stupid as she would kiss him to show sincerity or some such nonsense. He had kept her from making things so much worse and embarrassing. It didn't lessen the fact that he *knew* that she *knew* that he *knew*. And there she was in a muddled mess again by his mere presence in her life.

"It's just a lunch. Surrounded by many other people. Your reputation will remain intact by being seen with me, a rodeo cowboy, in a group of diners...just dining." The look and grin coupled with the triple threat of the gleam in the blue eyes... What else could she say? *Get it over with.*

"If I do, you will go away?"

He nodded.

"Fine. I'll let Mel know. Be right back."

FINE. THAT WAS full of excitement...*not.* More like someone giving in to having a root canal. Somehow this was one female that could easily damage his male ego if he wasn't careful to keep on guard. And he'd have to do a lot better at doing that instead of buying a gift and putting a bow on it and then forgetting his resolution to stay as far away from Laurie Wilkes as possible. The lunch idea just popped out of his mouth and that was that. *Just lunch.* Then they were done.

Twenty minutes later they were seated in the shade of a brightly striped hot pink and lime green canopy over a table on the patio of The Back Porch, a restaurant attached to the famous Yellow Rose Dance Hall, the oldest dance hall in the state of Texas. An icon known far and wide for toe-tapping music for dancing, good clean fun for the entire family, great food, and a romantic bed-and-breakfast.

"I didn't expect to be lunching here. I assumed it would be a burger at the diner." Laurie opened the menu and glanced down it.

"Well, it's too nice a day to be stuck inside. Have you been here before?"

She shook her head. "No, I haven't. I've wanted to since we returned but haven't taken the time. We would often come to the dances over in the dance hall when I was growing up. I remember listening to George Strait, Brad Paisley, Willie... You name it. It was a great memory of childhood. When we moved to Faris, I didn't come as often. Then I went off to college and that was it until today."

"Then I'm glad I decided on this. It's nice to be part of someone's first time." He flashed a grin, and she hoped the flush she felt crossing her cheeks was not that noticeable. It was not easy to decide if Trey said the things he did out of his quick wit or on purpose to get a rise out of her. She wasn't a prude, but she wasn't experienced in the flippant comment department.

The food had been ordered, the teas delivered, and their salads were set before them all in short order. She picked up her fork and began on the salad. A tall, beautiful blonde with long hair and gorgeous skin stopped by the table. Her smile was full on Trey. He was on his feet in one movement and they embraced. Laurie felt the old feelings of being the "girl in the corner" surface, and she quickly tapped them down.

She was an adult with a decent life and a beautiful child and what else would matter?

Trey turned toward Laurie and made introductions. "Laurie Wilkes, I'd like you to meet Lily Rose. She is one of the Rose sisters who own this wonderful property. The gardens which we'll visit after our lunch are all her handiwork. She has the greenest thumb in the state of Texas."

"It's lovely to meet you, Laurie," the woman spoke first in warm, welcoming tones, and she extended her hand. Laurie responded in kind. "I'm so happy that you and Trey stopped by today. We haven't seen this cowboy out on the dance floor in a very long time. Perhaps you can talk him into coming more often and not just for lunch."

"Laurie is taking care of the general store in town for her grandfather this summer. She was telling me she used to come here for dances in her youth."

"That's wonderful. I love going into that store and finding all sorts of things that I never knew I needed," she replied with a laugh. Laurie was finding it hard to not like the woman. She seemed to be a genuine person who just happened to be gorgeous. And it was clear she and Trey were friends and nothing else. "I'll look forward to stopping in now and visiting a bit with you. I did see you've added more plants recently and I am always in need of more of those…in case you can't tell." They all shared a laugh on that comment given the massive presence on the patios of potted flowers and planted shrubs.

"I'll leave you both to enjoy your meal and do take a stroll through the gardens. I'd love to hear what you think about them, Laurie." She left them and Trey returned to his seat.

"She seems very nice."

"All three of the sisters are. Jazz usually runs the restaurant, and Lily takes care of the gardens and the bed-and-breakfast. Calla is the oldest sister; she takes care of the overall business end of things and is an attorney in town and married to your county judge."

"Really? I didn't know that. But I usually am not wired into the town's gossip hotline."

"Well, that might not be bad at that. We met them when my family joined with them to put on a rodeo to help celebrate the designation of the dance hall being made a historical building by the state. It coincided with the anniversary of the founding of McKenna Springs, so it was a big celebration about three or four years ago now."

"Your family is quite well-known in these parts." Then she fell silent for a moment, contemplating the words she wanted to put out there. Trey was watching her.

"And what's on your mind right now that you seem to hesitate over?"

How could he know her so well at times? "I heard about the tragedy in your family while I was living in Dallas. I'm terribly sorry for you and your siblings. I can't imagine how awful a time it was...and will probably continue to be for a very long time. And I'm sorry if you don't like to have it brought up."

There was a pause as the waitress brought their entrees to the table. Once she walked away, Trey nodded. "I appreciate your comment. And I guess we've learned to live with it every day that it doesn't bother us to have people mention it. They were good people, loved by many, and we miss them daily and always will. So no, I don't mind you saying what you did." He fell silent, his fork pushing around the food on his plate for a moment. Laurie felt his pain was not that far below the surface.

"Tell me about your siblings and the rodeo business. I am a novice and know nothing. I will own that for a fact."

His face brightened, and that made her feel pleased. "Well, first, forget the tabloids. They don't deal in facts. The lies they manufacture are a lot more interesting than reality so that's their bread and butter. If you want to know about rodeo, then you go to a few and talk to the people who run them, ride in them, and live them every day.

"Guess I should begin with our family. There's Aunt Sal who is more like the patriarch and matriarch all rolled into one. She was Mom's sister, and we don't know what we would have done without her over these last few years in keeping us together and headed down the road without stumbling.

"Thomas is the oldest. He married a sweet lady named Jamie a couple years ago and they have a son, Andy. He's a great little guy...a regular cowboy, who for some reason wants to follow in his uncle Trey's footsteps," he said with a pleased grin. "And Thomas and Jamie just had their little daughter, Taylor, about three months ago.

"Then you have Truitt, who just got married to Annie, and they have a daughter named Jamie, who is about thirteen now. Jamie is technically Truitt's sister-in-law, but it's complicated." He shook his head. "They are growing up too fast on me. And then I am next in line after Truitt. And last but far from least, is our sister Tori. She's one of a kind. She speaks her mind on any and every subject, is the energy behind this whole stock producing for rodeos and has been courted since second grade by our county sheriff. She's stubborn, and he's determined is how I describe it. And there you have the update on the Tremayne clan."

She shook her head. "It sounds like quite a family. I can tell you obviously are proud of them all. I can hear it in your voice. But what about *your* part in all of that? You glossed over that in a hurry. Tell me about who the Trey Tremayne sitting in front of me really is...since you think I've heard it all wrong." She crossed her arms on the table in front of her and gave her total concentration to the man who fell quiet. So much so that she thought he planned to just ignore her question. After several long moments, he gave in.

"Things pretty much can be divided into two parts in our family. The part before the accident, and the part after it. After we lost our parents and little brother, and Truitt lost his fiancée…we took a while to find our way. As a young person, you figure your parents will always be there…at least for a few decades. But then they aren't, and life gets real…really fast. My brother Thomas was thrust into running a huge ranch literally overnight. Thankfully, he had Pops to help him. Pops is like a grandpa and trusted head foreman all rolled into one. Truitt had to set aside his pain and do what he could to help out. Tori and I were younger, but we kinda clung together and hung on as best as we could. Seemed we all evolved after that. Everyone seemed to have a perfect niche carved for themselves. I realized I might need to go out in search of mine. I graduated early and hit the rodeo road."

"And you discovered you were good at it." She smiled to encourage him to continue.

"Well, it took a few bumps and broken limbs, but yeah…I eventually became really good at it. And the bright lights and shiny belt buckles and adrenaline rushes every night…well, those can make you forget a lot of things. And when the tabloids and press want to make you into something a lot more interesting than you might be, you shrug and go along with it. You should never believe your own press though. That's a hard lesson for rookies to learn."

"Especially where all those female fans are concerned? I remember one headline of one of those rags I saw at the pharmacy called you 'rodeo's sexy stud buster' or some such poetic prose. So, you are telling me that you didn't earn that title?"

Trey looked at her in silence, and when he responded, there wasn't the usual grin in sight.

"There might have been a couple of years in there when I enjoyed the attention of the fairer sex. And that is something I'm not proud of, but I did manage to outgrow that particular stage. There came a time when it became not so much about fun and excitement but a serious business you had to keep your head in the game with or lose it." There was a slight upturn of a corner of his mouth. "Of course, I might like to point out that it could have also been that I matured and became a responsible adult but then that wouldn't be as exciting reading about in those tabloids, now would it?"

"I suppose not. And I might have to revise some of my previous misconceptions about you in that case. I suppose it can become a normal way of life if one is always hiding behind a facade that is not reality. And you can't help being a red-blooded male when those little cowgirls want to throw themselves at you."

He shook his head. "I somehow feel like I might be headed into a minefield here. But it's a little late for me to apologize for being one of those males you speak about. I can only hope that you take the man seated in front of you right now at face value. And you were right to whittle me down to size that first day. I can apologize again, but I also feel like I can speak up enough with you to put something on the table that has me mystified and off-balance a bit with you."

"I'm intrigued, so I will *try* to temper any reaction I

might have as you lay whatever this is on the table between us. Did that come out right?"

"No turning back now," Trey grinned in response. "I can't quite figure you out. And that *isn't* a bad thing," he said, holding up a hand to allow himself to continue. "When I say that you aren't like most of the other women I've come across, please know that *is* a compliment. And you already know that I think you are a very good mother. T.J. is an awesome kid.

"But you have this way of cutting through the BS and saying what you mean. And you expect the same in return. Only that's something I might have to practice more as I wouldn't want you to think I'm flirting for the heck of it or using a line on you or whatever. I *like* you, Laurie Wilkes. You're like this breath of that fresh air that rushes in the open window of your truck and you settle back and enjoy the open road on a perfect Texas afternoon…not too hot, not too cold…just right. And that sounds like the worst possible compliment. See? *That* is what happens when I say it straight out and don't add the usual 'flirty' rodeo stud vocabulary."

Something went all "marshmallow-gooey" inside of her as he brought the words out. That was the best description she could muster at the moment…thanks to her son having used it when he was younger. This cowboy was turning the tables on all her preconceived ideas about him. And turning that wall she had thrown up between them into a very flimsy curtain at best.

"I think that's enough to render you speechless and me, too. It's probably time to suggest we walk off some of the excellent lunch we just had. Let's take a tour of some of those gardens." He slid his chair back and stood. Laurie felt relief that a response from her to what all he had just said was not expected in that moment. She nodded her head and soon they were walking down the stone pathways that traversed the fragrant gardens in masses of roses in a variety of colors, hedges of colorful blooms and fragrances that mixed and mingled—freesia, jasmine, honeysuckle and more. There were water features sprinkled here and there and benches where people could sit a spell and take it all in. Beside a pond filled with bright koi swimming around its clear waters, they found a spot to sit and watch them for a few minutes.

"I see by the smile on your face the last few minutes that you find the gardens of the Yellow Rose to your liking?"

"It's amazing what Lily and her sisters have done here. I had no idea, or I would have come to visit sooner. It's a beautiful oasis. Thank you for having such a nice idea to come here."

Trey nodded. "I'm glad you like it. And since you thought this was a good idea, I hope you'll think my next idea is the same."

That caught Laurie's attention in a heartbeat. What was on this cowboy's mind next?

"I'm almost afraid to ask what it is. But since you did

have this good idea, I'm willing to keep an open mind. Shoot."

"The other night at dinner, T.J. was telling me about his scout group and the different things that they have done, places they visit, and all that. I had an idea. One of the things that my family and I are becoming involved in and hope to develop into a permanent part of our ranch is to have a program for young people who want to learn how to be successful in the sport of rodeo. We'll have classes for them in several areas…roping, bull riding, broncs…and more. That way we can keep the sport alive and interest more young people into carrying it forward. But all that aside, I thought it might be something different and fun to offer to bring out the scout group to the ranch for an afternoon rodeo and barbecue. I didn't want to mention it to T.J. or anyone else until I ran it by you and got your opinion on it first."

Laurie sat for a few long moments trying to gather all the information he had just spun out for her into some sort of order. It was apparent that this was something that was very important to him.

"Sounds like you've given this some serious thought."

His smile was broad and made her feel all that warmth inside again. "I have. Although for a little while, when you and I were not exactly on the best of terms, I was afraid that I might just have to shelve it all. But now, I think it's too good an idea for the kids not to have a chance to enjoy something at the ranch. I know my family would love to have them come out."

"When did you think would be a good time to do this?"

"How about Sunday? Think T.J. would be down for some rodeo stuff and a swim in the afternoon…some good barbecue thrown in for energy?"

His response caught her by surprise. "So soon? You *have* been giving this a lot of thought. But why is it so important that you wanted me to give my stamp of approval first?"

"Because first and foremost, this is an invitation to also have you and T.J. be my guests at the ranch and enjoy it. The fact that we can share it with his friends in his troop and teach them some things about rodeo and animals and such, well that is just another layer of icing on the cake. But I wouldn't bring it up to anyone else if you thought it wasn't a sound idea and you weren't comfortable with it. I know you have some misgivings about me spending time around T.J. and I…"

"I was wrong." She stopped him. "That was me before I opened my mind and listened to a mature version of Trey Tremayne talk about rodeo. Now I have been enlightened…somewhat. And I do think the kids would get a lot out of what you are planning. So don't let me stand in the way."

"Well, I might have left out the part where you are invited along, too. I figure we need parental chaperones with fifteen kids coming out. And I'd like you to see the ranch and meet my family, too? That is, if you want to."

Laurie slowly shook her head. "You never cease to amaze me with how your mind works at times. How do you do that? I bet you were the one in the family who always had a way out of every bit of trouble you stepped into."

"And you are good at sidestepping my question, Laurie Wilkes. How about it?"

"In the interest of *education*, how could I stand in the way of such an offer?"

"I've always said you can't have too much education." He grinned as she raised an eyebrow, reminding him that she had seen how he behaved in school and that was as fake a statement as a two-dollar bill given his past. "It will be a day to remember."

Chapter Seven

A DAY TO *remember.* Trey shook his head. He was heading into McKenna Springs. He planned to grab a quick breakfast taco at the diner and then be on time to pick up Laurie and T.J. So much for his determination to end things with the pair…before he decided it wouldn't hurt to wait until after a nice lunch for two. And then he had blurted out the idea of taking them to the ranch…just an educational experience for T.J.'s scout troop. *Right.*

Somehow, he was losing his good sense. Whatever it was, he was treading on thin ice with this all day, hosting the woman and her son. At least he could count on his family. When he had casually dropped the news into the conversation around the dinner table at Aunt Sal's that evening after having lunch with Laurie, there had been a moment of silence.

Maybe more than a moment. Of course, his sister Tori had to be the first to chime in. *"Wait a minute. Trey Tremayne is now dating a mother with a young, impressionable son? Does she not know who you are? Mr. Love 'Em and Leave 'Em of the rodeo circuit? Did that bronc hit your head by mistake?"*

"Tori." Thomas threw their sister a look and his tone was meant to temper the rest of whatever she might say. "It's good that you're taking the time to share rodeo with those youngsters. You're very good with young people. Look how much your young nephews and nieces follow in your shadow."

"Perhaps because you relate so well on their mental level?" Tori couldn't help the fast jab. She smiled sweetly and went back to her dessert. He had waited for Truitt to chime in, but he just kept his attention on the meal in front of him. Aunt Sal smiled and said that she would be happy to see that they had a lovely lunch for their visitors, and she knew everyone would be happy to greet them and make them feel welcome. With that, she had spoken, and all would take heed.

"Well, you're here early enough," Darcy commented as he strode through the door of the diner and chose a seat at the counter. "And I seem to have heard from a certain excited youngster last evening that you're turning into a tour guide of sorts. Can that be right?"

"Why am I not surprised you've heard about the field trip to educate people on rodeo and ranching and all such things? And in addition to this coffee, I'll take one of your special breakfast tacos." He took the coffee mug in hand she had sat in front of him and took a sip.

"This is for educational purposes. I do believe I heard that mentioned also." She gave him a level look, and he could see the gleam of mirth in her eyes.

"Go ahead and laugh. I've already had that from my sister."

Darcy nodded. "That is why I will tell you that I think it will mean a lot to T.J. And then I will also tell you that I hope you realize that Laurie isn't your usual type of girl. Try to keep that in mind. And that's my two cents." She reached for the taco that the cook placed in the serving window behind her. "Enjoy your breakfast."

"Hey, Darcy," he spoke up as the woman turned away. She gave him her attention again. "Why do you think I have a certain 'type' of girl?"

"You want me to shoot straight with you?"

"I wouldn't have asked you otherwise."

"We both know how you attract the buckle bunnies. You have an attitude about you that you love living on the edge, being footloose and fancy free, and you take off down the road to your rodeos without a glance behind you. You are a celebrity and like the spotlight. Sometimes people can't take you seriously because it seems you don't do that, either. You're a great guy, but maybe a girl like Laurie...a single mom who has had to deal with some hard knocks in her life and take care of a child and herself...well, maybe she needs someone who sticks around and has a strong enough shoulder for two at times. You've got to want to be a partner 24/7. And rodeo can't last forever. Then what?" Darcy shook her head. "Guess that was a bit more than you expected. Just don't play loose with feelings when it comes to these two people. They're special and deserve more." She turned away and left him to eat in peace. And to digest her words. Somehow his appetite wasn't as hearty as he thought when he walked in the door.

He replayed several things about what his family had said and what Darcy had said, and there were things that he needed to really give some thought to. But the clock was ticking and there were two people waiting on him. He took the final two bites of taco and emptied the coffee mug. He waved to Darcy who was across the room pouring another customer a cup of coffee as he headed to the door.

As his truck made the corner onto the main street, he spotted a familiar figure standing on the porch in front of the store. Trey smiled. The boy was obviously anxious for his arrival, and the grin that broke across his face as Trey pulled into the parking space in front of him couldn't have been any broader. T.J. was dressed in jeans and a blue and white striped T-shirt. A baseball cap with the Dallas Cowboys emblem was on his head. Trey swung out of the truck and mounted the steps to the porch.

"I can see you're ready. Is your mom ready, too?"

"She's getting the bag with our swim stuff and all. We almost forgot it."

"Well, that wouldn't have been good. The swimming part is one of the best things about today."

"I'm sorry I kept you waiting."

Trey looked up, and he found himself taking a deeper

breath before responding. For whatever reason, her appearance as she stepped outside the door to join them caught him up short. He managed to step forward and take the bag from her. "You're right on time. Let's load up and get our day started. We should be there ahead of the arrival of the rest of the troop members and their parents."

He held the door open for her to take the passenger side seat. As she passed in front of him, a light scent of something sweet and memorable filtered through his senses. Trey smiled and stayed quiet. He next made certain that T.J. was settled and buckled up in the back seat. The bag went on the seat next to him. Trey walked around and slid into the driver's seat, his brain still trying to catch up and figure what felt different about the moment.

IT WAS A twenty-minute drive from McKenna Springs into Faris. Then it was another ten-minute ride out of town to the ranch gates. During the drive, Laurie was both thankful to her son and confused. There was something about Trey's demeanor that she couldn't put her finger on. From the moment she had stepped onto the porch, she had sensed that something wasn't quite the norm with him. He smiled and he answered T.J.'s myriad of questions with patience and some humor but she couldn't pinpoint it. Had she done something? Had she dressed wrong? She was wearing a fairly new pair of jeans; the top was a fitted camisole of white eyelet material with wide ruffles on the shoulder straps and tiny pearl-type buttons down the front. It was sleeveless and the neckline was square. It showed off the light tan she had managed to attain so far that summer. She wore a pair of sneakers, having freed herself of the heavy boot. She had left her hair to hang loose around her shoulders, and there was a scrunchy in her pocket in case the heat got too much, so she could put it up into a ponytail. Tiny gold studs were her only jewelry. Laurie just remained outwardly smiling and content to listen to the conversation around her and take in the scenery outside her window.

As they crossed the metal cattle guard beneath the arched iron ranch gate emblazoned with the brand and name of the Four T Ranch, she sat up straighter, aware of the butterflies of nervousness taking flight in her stomach. She had no idea what type of reception she and T.J. would receive from the rest of the Tremaynes. From what she had gleaned last evening in the diner from a conversation with Darcy, this ranch dated back to the 1800s and covered a few hundred thousand acres. It was a huge deal, and the Tremaynes were held in very high esteem.

"If we take the road ahead to the right, we would be headed to Thomas and Jamie's home. Thomas oversees the daily operations of the whole ranch, but in particular the cattle business which is housed in this section of the ranch. We are going straight ahead, and we'll turn to the left in another half mile. Then we'll be where I live in the main ranch headquarters along with Aunt Sal. Truitt was there with us until he and Annie just finished their own home about three miles farther north on the ranch. Tori lives in her own small house closer to the rodeo stock pens and the office for those operations."

"So each person has their own home on the ranch. You are close but still far enough apart," she observed.

"Yes. It's good we're a close family, but we all have our separate things we are involved in under the umbrella of the ranch itself. I am on the road half of the year, so it made sense just to stay in one of the bedrooms of the family's main house. One day, if anyone takes me on, then I've got my eye on a really pretty bit of land on a hilltop a couple of miles away."

"And if your partner doesn't like it the same way?" She ventured to put that thought out there.

"Then I guess we wouldn't be all that compatible after all," he replied easily enough. "It's not that she wouldn't have the right to her opinion or anything, but I would hope to find someone who has much the same tastes and outlook on things. From what I've seen of my brothers' marriages and before that, my parents' marriage, that seems to be the best course for a happy union. But who knows?"

Laurie fell quiet as they came in sight of the large three-story, sprawling home with its wide porches and balconies. It was beautiful. When she was younger, just growing up, she often daydreamed about such a home. The Tremaynes were truly lucky to have such a place to call home. The engine shut off, and Laurie and T.J. exited the truck as Trey did. They waited until he had the bag in hand, and then they walked beside him up the walkway and the steps to the porch. They had just reached the top when the door was thrown open and a tall lady with silver hair stepped out with a warm smile on her face.

"Welcome! I got caught up in the kitchen or I would have been out here as soon as you pulled up. I'm Sallie Lomax. But everyone calls me Aunt Sal, and you are welcome to do that also."

"Thank you," Laurie smiled in return, the butterflies settling a bit. "I'm Laurie and this is T.J." The young boy remembered his manners and held out his hand. Aunt Sal beamed at him and returned the handshake.

"That's a good handshake, young man. I appreciate that. But don't stand out here; come on in and make yourselves at home. How about some iced tea or soda? Cold milk?"

"Iced tea would be nice," Laurie responded, "and a soda would be fine for T.J....whatever you have."

"Trey, put the bag in the pink room upstairs. Thomas and Jamie and the kids will be here shortly," she said. She added, turning to Laurie, "They just had a new one not too long ago, and they are finding out about the joys of packing for a major move with a baby in tow even though you are just going a couple of miles." She laughed and Laurie nodded in agreement.

"Their son, Andy, is a year or so older than your age I believe, T.J. You two should hit it off. Truitt is already down at the arena getting things set up there along with some of the hands. They'll park the rest of the visitors closer to the arena. Pops is in his usual place among the barbecue pits and such. Annie and Jamie are out in the kitchen, helping with getting the other things put together for lunch. And that, I believe, is the rundown."

They headed toward the hallway just as the front door opened. A young woman with the same blue eyes as the other Tremaynes came in with the breeze, her reddish-blond hair swept into a ponytail. "You're forgetting the best part of the family roll call." The young woman looked at Laurie with a grin on her face. "But then they like to save the best for last around here." She stuck out her hand. "I'm Tori, the precious sweet baby of the family."

Laurie stifled a laugh, but it still came out as a wide grin as she took the offered hand. "I do believe I have heard that description before."

"Not from me," Trey spoke, rounding the corner from the staircase and shooting his sister a brotherly smirk.

"And your nose is growing," Tori responded right back. "Iced tea sounds good. Let's take this party into the kitchen."

More introductions were made in the kitchen while Aunt Sal poured the drinks. Annie was Truitt's wife of less than a year, and Jamie was her little sister, and two or three years older than Andy and T.J. She soon had T.J. seated on a barstool close by where she was cutting pickles for the relish tray. She had engaged him in the usual conversation starters: what grade, favorite subject, sport, etc. Laurie was glad to see a usually quiet around strangers T.J. was opening up readily enough.

Laurie was given a seat on another barstool and she was aware that Trey stayed close by…not hovering but supportive. She appreciated that. Whenever she caught his eye, he would smile or nod, and once he even threw her a look that made her foot miss the bar on the bottom of her stool and she had to recover her balance quickly. It seemed that no one noticed, and she was grateful for that. She tried not to look in his direction again.

"I think while we're waiting for the arena to be ready and the others to arrive, this might be a good time for me to do my presentation on this field trip as you call it and introduce Laurie and T.J. to *my* babies. Up for a little road trip over to my place?" She looked at Laurie, who responded with a nod. "Then let's go. Trey you can stay and help Truitt and the guys. And be extra careful with…"

Trey put his hands up. "I know, I know… Be careful with Doodlebug and Milkshake. I wouldn't dare do otherwise with those two."

She laughed and guided the pair out the back door and down to where another truck sat with the same ranch logo on its doors as Trey's had. As they pulled away from the house, Laurie couldn't help herself. "Doodlebug and Milkshake? Is that code or something?"

Tori laughed and shook her head. "They are two of my babies. I raise bucking bulls for rodeos. We are giving these two guys a go today in the arena with our cowboys to see how they are coming along."

Laurie was silent for a moment. "You raise bulls? Is that normal...or I mean is it a usual thing..."

"A usual thing for a girl to do?" Tori smiled. "It's a very typical question that I get when people first hear about it. No, it's not typical because there are maybe four or five of us females in the country who truly do this. Fewer than that that have bulls on the national pro circuit."

"And you do?"

"If Trey were here, I'd knock on his head for something wooden to ward off bad luck." She grinned over her shoulder at a laughing T.J. "So far, my bulls are on schedule to hopefully compete at the national championships in a year or two. Right now, they are racking up points...which means how they perform and how many cowboys can't stay on them for a full eight-second ride. One day, one of my bulls will be the best of the best."

"No brag, just fact," Laurie supplied and earned another big smile and nod of the head.

They passed a lovely, smaller brick home with an inviting front porch with rocking chairs, potted plants, and a tin roof under the shade of a couple of pecan trees. Tori pointed to it as they moved past toward a set of barns and activity in pens. "That's my home back there. I get to see it once in a while when I am not on the road with the rodeo stock and Trey." She pulled in and stopped beside one of the pens. The trio got out and moved to the fence.

"Man, what is that?" T.J. spoke in an awed whisper as he pointed toward the animal inside the penned area.

Laurie had never seen such a mass of beef and horns. And when the animal turned its massive head in her direction, she involuntarily took a step backward.

Tori nodded at him and in a voice full of pride, made the introductions. "This incredible creature is my pride and joy, Maximus. He's the one who is going to be the top bucking bull in the not-too-distant future."

"Cowboys actually want to get on his back? Are they just insane?" Laurie could only stand and look back at the animal watching them.

"They get on him, but so far, none have stayed. That is what makes him gold. But to me, he is still the orphan I hand-raised when we lost his mom to a gopher hole and infection set in." She reached inside her pocket and put something in her palm. She put her lower arm through the fence posts. Laurie thought she had to be crazy.

Slowly, the animal moved toward her, then flicked out a long tongue and the lemon candy was gone. She would never have believed it if she hadn't seen it.

"You actually have that massive animal eating out of the

palm of your hand, while cowboys end up being launched into outer space by the same bull. Incredible."

"I can't explain it, but the bulls have always fascinated me. I respect their size and their power. While they are small, I walk among them and try hard not to get too attached to them, but it is a losing battle. As they get older, I stay a distance from them and that is hard. But each one is my baby and I try to raise them to be the best...much the same as a human mom does, I would think."

Laurie nodded. "It might be strange, but I get what you're saying. I hope your babies all grow up to not like cowboys." They both burst out laughing. A friendship was being forged.

They were just about to get back in the truck to return to the ranch when a marked law enforcement vehicle pulled up next to them, and the driver's window rolled down. A very good-looking man in a uniform, hat on head, and sunshades removed as he nodded hello, smiled at the three of them. Tori made the introductions.

"This is Sheriff Gray Dalton. Gray this is Laurie Wilkes and her son, T.J. They are friends of Trey's and visiting us for the day. I suppose you're working today?"

He spoke to Laurie and T.J. and then placed his gaze on Tori. "And you would be wrong. When I heard that Pops was putting on a barbecue, how could I possibly skip that sort of invite...from your aunt Sal. She cares about me."

Laurie remembered Trey telling her about Tori and her

elementary school romance. This had to be the little boy all grown up. Was the woman blind?

"Don't let us keep you from the food." Tori moved to the truck, and Laurie smiled at the man who nodded in return and then followed. There was a story there, but she doubted it would be told by Tori to anyone. Laurie didn't understand why finding romance had to be so difficult for some and easy for others.

Chapter Eight

"DO YOU NORMALLY do this every weekend? I thought I heard a woman mention that earlier in the stands." Laurie leaned closer to Trey to be heard over the noise in the arena. The structure was really state-of-the-art as far as her meager experience could tell. But it was a huge arena with a metal roof and sides that could be opened on all four sides to allow the breezes and people to come and go. Or closed to make an indoor arena facility that could be heated, and climate controlled in less hospitable weather. There were chutes on both ends and comfortable stadium seating ran the length of both sides. There was even an announcer's box and areas for judges and cowboys waiting for their rides.

Trey shook his head. "Not every weekend. We hold auctions of some of our livestock in here; we let area schools come in and use it for their animal husbandry programs or benefit rodeos, that sort of thing. We built this with the rodeo school in mind. Too many of the youngsters coming along now don't really know the right and wrong ways of doing things. They end up getting seriously hurt or doing

DEBRA HOLT

damage to the animals or whatever. It'd be a way for us to pay it forward for the opportunities the sport has provided us over the years. But that's still in the planning stages for when we hang up our spurs so to speak." He grinned at the thought. Laurie had to wonder if someone like Trey could ever do that willingly. But she applauded what he wanted to do for young people.

"And today? What is this about today? Besides being a field trip for the scouts who look like they are all having a ton of fun so far." There was a lot of horses and cowboys and cattle and more coming and going in the chutes and pens. And the stands had a good amount of people settling in to watch whatever was about to happen, in addition to the two dozen or so people invited by T.J. at Trey's behest.

"Today is about you and T.J." The matter-of-fact statement gave her a shock. She looked at him and tried to see if he was joking in some way.

"About us? Come on, what's the real reason?"

"Seriously…I asked the team if as long as we needed to run some green stock through the paces, why couldn't we do it today? Add some good food and make it a fun play day for one and all. Then the idea of adding in the scout troop to use some of this in its educational context, well that was a no-brainer. And the people you see gathering in here are family members of the ranch hands who work on the Four T properties. And since this is about sharing rodeo with some green horns…excuse me, dial down that spitfire you're about to throw at me…or I could say tenderfoot…if you like that better? But you and T.J. can get a flavor for what a much larger, more competitive rodeo would be comprised of. So you just sit back and relax. I have some things to do right now, but my sisters-in-law and Pops and Aunt Sal will be around you to answer any questions and fill you in on what's happening. Enjoy." He shot her a departing smile and a wink and then she watched him amble off through the bleachers.

"Enjoying yourself so far?" Aunt Sal scooted over to take the spot Trey had filled.

"Yes, we are. There is so much to see and do. Tori showed us her 'babies' this morning and now we have this. I just hope you all didn't go to a lot of trouble today."

"Don't fret about that. This family will take every opportunity to compete against each other."

"Each other?"

"Thomas and Truitt will be doing some team roping. Then they'll split up and go at each other in bulldogging and steer roping. Tori's going to put some of her young bulls out there for the novice cowboys in the area to give it a shot and see if they truly want to make bull riding their sport. She's up there on the catwalk overseeing the whole show with some interns from an area university who want to learn the ins and outs of rodeo production. If Trey wasn't still on the mend, he'd be on a bronc or two today. And Tori may even do some barrels today. She still is a darn good trainer of barrel horses. I wish she'd get into that more, but she has her dream to accomplish first."

"This is amazing. I love how you're encouraging the young people to get involved and be able to pass it on to the next generation."

Aunt Sal nodded her head to the five kids lined up at the railing, their legs dangling over the edge, eyes glued to the activity before them. "Those are the next generation coming along. Andy is already getting into roping and such with Thomas and Truitt. Jamie is learning to be a competitor in showing horses in the ring and working with training ranch horses with Truitt. Their friends lined up down there with them are all from ranching families and involved in one form or another."

Laurie's gaze fell on T.J. who watched every move in the arena with intense interest. He was loving every moment of the day.

"Excuse me, ladies." Trey had walked up and nodded in Laurie's direction. "Could I talk to you for a moment over by the gate?"

Laurie stood and then slid under the railing, a short hop and she was beside him. His hand shot out to steady her. It didn't drop from her elbow as they walked a few steps away just beyond the viewing stands.

"What's up?"

"There's a portion of smaller rodeos where the young-sters in attendance get a chance to get into the arena and the action. It's called mutton busting. We have all ages…from toddlers who can barely walk up to age twelve. We put them on large sheep, put a helmet on them for safety, and then they come out of the gate and hold on for dear life. Those who make it for the full ride, advance into the finals. Then those kids go again, and the winner gets a trophy and gift certificate to the local western wear store. It's fun and they enjoy it. The kids will all be joining in, and I wanted to get your permission to ask T.J. if he'd like to join in, too. What do you think?"

"He's never been around a sheep even," she said. "And if he fell off…"

"He'd get up and keep going like the rest of the kids. I think he'd enjoy the experience. I wouldn't suggest anything I thought might hurt him."

She met his gaze, and she knew that was a truth she could take to the bank. Everything else aside, she had seen how Trey was a genuine Pied Piper around the younger set. They followed him with rapt attention, and he was a natural with them. She nodded. "If he wants to do it, then it's fine with me."

That earned one of his grins that did those funny things to her pulse, and she allowed her gaze to meet his for a few long moments. His gaze moved to settle on her lips, and she tried to keep breathing in the midst of the sudden desire to feel what a kiss might be like from this cowboy. And that thought shocked her into silence.

"Hey, Mom! Can I go with Andy to get some popcorn?" The voice was enough to break the moment, and Trey's hand dropped from her elbow and the air moved back into her lungs. She turned to see the pair approaching. "Sure, no problem."

"But first, I have some business to conduct with you two young men. How about I treat you guys to the popcorn and fill you in on something I have in mind that you might have some fun with?" Both heads nodded with emphasis. Trey shot her a departing look that might have had a promise to get back to their previous conversation at some point in the not-too-distant future, but then maybe she was just being fanciful. She watched the trio, tall cowboy in the middle, head off toward the concession stand.

Thirty minutes later, T.J. came running toward her as she stood at the gate of the arena. "Did you see that Mom? Wasn't that awesome?" She helped him take off the helmet and the number pinned to the back of his shirt. Laurie hadn't seen her son so ecstatic over something in a very long while. "Thanks for letting me do it, Trey."

Laurie looked up and Trey had come to stand behind her, a grin on his face as he nodded at the boy. "Fine job, for your first time. Let's head back to the house and get ready for some food and then swimming. You earned it, cowboy." He withdrew the hand from behind his back, and Laurie saw the straw cowboy hat. He placed it on T.J.'s head. "That looks pretty good on you. What do you think? Consider it a belated birthday gift."

"Wow, a real cowboy hat like Andy's and yours and all the other guys. What do you think, Mom?"

Laurie felt two male gazes on her and waiting for her reaction. She smiled. "I think first and foremost you should remember your manners, my son."

T.J. swung his attention back to the cowboy. "Thanks a bunch, Trey. It's the best gift ever. I'll wear it all the time. I look like Andy and the others now."

"Let's get back to the house so you can get some of that sheep smell off of you, too," Laurie pointed out, glad she had packed extra clothing for after the swimming pool. Her son definitely needed some time with soap and hot water.

"Last one to the truck is a rotten egg." T.J. didn't wait on them. Trey fell into step beside her at a more sedate pace.

"Thank you, Trey. For making this such an unforgettable experience for T.J. He'll have a lot to write about when he gets back to school in Dallas, and the teacher tells them to write about what they did on their summer vacation."

She sensed a slight change in the man beside her. Laurie ventured a glance up at him, and the smile had faded into a thoughtful countenance.

"Summer vacation," the words were sort of rolled around on his tongue as he spoke them. "I guess I had forgotten for a bit about you saying you were just here to help out your grandfather while he was away on his honeymoon in Florida. I suppose it slipped my mind that one of these days, you and your son would have to return to your other life."

Somehow when he spoke the words aloud, they didn't sound as positive as they once had. It was true. Their summer would come to an end, and their lives were waiting for them back in Dallas. "I never liked the ending of summer," Trey said. Laurie stayed silent.

Pops had outdone himself on the brisket and sausages he had barbecued in the huge pits for their meal. Long tables had been spread out on the front lawn of the house, under the shade of the half dozen or so pecan and oak trees, their sprawling limbs providing cooling shade for the diners. Serving bowls of potato salad, coleslaw, beans, and loaves of homemade bread sat family-style on the tables. Iced tea in pitchers, sodas, and bottles of ice-cold adult beverages filled silver tubs full of ice. Smaller tables held pies and larger pans of banana pudding and cobblers. Laurie took it all in and simply shook her head in amazement.

Between Aunt Sal and Jamie and Annie, she had been introduced to what she felt had to be all the residents of Faris, Texas. When she realized that most of the people were just those who worked on the ranch and their families, and a few special guests from town like the sheriff and a few others, she shook her head and gave up trying to remember all the names and faces. What was even more amazing to her was how each person seemed to be genuine in their welcome and concerned that she and T.J. were made to feel welcome and were having a good time.

Trey was the perfect host, as well. He was very attentive to both her and T.J. They were seated at the table with his siblings and their families, and she was amazed at how easy it was to join in the conversations. T.J. and Andy and Jamie had evidently formed their own small trio.

"I can't. I just can't eat one more bite." Laurie shook her head as she pushed away her plate. "It is so incredibly good, but I am going to have to not eat for a week to compensate for all I have eaten today."

Trey grinned as his gaze slid over her in a most appreciative way. "I doubt you have to worry about anything. But it's nice to see a lady who doesn't eat like a bird and *then* says she must diet for a month."

"Which could be an offhanded compliment of sorts or a nice way to say I eat like a football player?" Laurie met his gaze but couldn't hold a straight face for very long. They both shared the laugh. That was something that had surprised her more than once over the last couple of hours. It was easy to smile and laugh with Trey Tremayne. He had a sense of humor that also he had no problem pointing at himself.

"Well, I would love a third helping of Aunt Sal's banana pudding, but I will do the wise thing and quit now." He finished with a swallow of tea and the crumpled napkin went onto the now empty plate. He folded his arms on the table in front of him and smiled at Laurie. "I don't know about you, but I think I need to take a walk right now. How about it?

We can take a tour of the stables and you can meet a couple of mares and their babies."

"Babies? Yes…that would be fun." She looked over where T.J. and the other kids were starting a game of football.

"I think he's too into the new friends he's made today to want to be taken away to go on a walk with a couple of old-timers like us." He stood up and waited for her decision.

She nodded and stood up, helping him gather their empty plates and glasses. They left them on the kitchen return tables and then set off down the small hill toward the red buildings with their silver roofs. It was a natural movement when her hand was captured in one of his as they walked side by side. Laurie didn't pull it back.

The stable he led them into was cavernous…or at least it seemed so to her, a novice in ranching. Three or four horses were inquisitive to see the visitors, and their heads turned and then moved to fill the open space of their stall doors. They stopped at the third stall, and Laurie looked on in amazement at the pair before them. A huge red horse, which she now could name as a bay in color, stood in the center of the stall and next to her, was a tiny miniature version of herself…only with a bright white blaze down its nose. The animal was mostly all spindly legs and huge bright eyes.

She moved to rest her hands on the top of the half-door. "Oh my goodness," Laurie breathed in admiration. "The baby is so beautiful. Is it a boy or girl?"

"She's a beautiful little girl…just like her mom. She was born a week ago, and they're doing fine."

"Does she have a name?"

"Callie's Little Bit of Red," he replied, glancing down at her. "That's her proper, on paper name. Jamie christened her Little Red so that's what she'll be called every day."

"You and your brothers and sister were blessed to be able to grow up in such an amazing place. It must be wonderful to be around so many beautiful animals, and the people are all so nice and friendly and the country…" She stopped. "I guess I got carried away there."

"Tell me about where Laurie Wilkes comes from. Your home is in Dallas? Do you have family there?"

She supposed it was only natural for him to be as inquisitive as she had been. "There isn't anything much to tell. Grandfather…my mother's father, is basically our family. I was an only child. My father worked himself into an early heart attack when I was ten. My mother had a stroke when I was eighteen. I used the insurance money and worked two jobs to put myself through college. Once I got my teaching degree, I went to work in Dallas, teaching first grade."

"That must mean you married young and had T.J. right after you graduated? That was a lot on your plate…new teacher, new wife, and new mom."

It was a simple observation, but Laurie felt the need to clarify a few points. For whatever reason, she felt she could share with this man the road she and T.J. traveled to become a family.

"T.J. came into my life when he was three years old. I'm not his birth mother. I lived next door to him and his dad, Jonathan Monroe. T.J.'s biological mom was killed in a car wreck when he was two. Jonathan and I were lifelines for each other…being neighbors in the same apartment complex. I would babysit when he had to work late to pick up shifts at his job, and he would keep my old car running each time it broke down so I could make it to classes and work. Then one day, after Jonathan had been sick with what we thought was a bad cold, he found out after some X-rays and a visit to a specialist, he was fighting lung cancer."

She paused, and Trey waited for her to continue when she was ready. "He came over one evening and said he was worried and had given a lot of thought to possible solutions. He had a half-sister that he didn't see very much and who wasn't someone he could see being a mother for T.J., given her lifestyle and the fact she hadn't been around in the last few years except when she needed money. He made the proposition then that since neither one of us had much of a family to rely upon, maybe we could make a family…if I was willing to take on the responsibility. He didn't have any other options. I thought a lot about it.

"In the end, I knew that I couldn't *not* agree to take care of that little boy. I had already fallen in love with him as he was such a good baby and a little charmer even then. So, we went down to the justice of peace one Monday morning and joined forces. It wasn't a love match. It was two good friends joining together to protect and care for a child that soon would be alone unless we could form a family. We did just that. Two months later, the cancer went into high gear, and in another three, Jonathan had died. So, if it seems odd to some people about how young a mom I must have been, that is the explanation that I don't often share."

"You were trying to get through college. And work to support your bills and schooling, and yet you didn't think twice about taking on the added challenge of raising a child. I have to say that I'm not surprised though. You were always the one who could be counted on. That was something I knew about you, even in school. You're an amazing lady with a huge heart and a heck of a lot of determination."

The way he said those words made her feel the weighted sincerity of each. "I think most people would have stepped forward in such a situation. It doesn't make me special or amazing. Although I do thank you for saying that."

"And you always were the least assuming person in the room. You did what was needed…including saving some of our lazy butts in literature and history classes along the way, writing papers for us and all…and never seemed to mind or seek out thanks." Trey's voice had lowered and there was something in his eyes that she couldn't make out. He seemed to have grown introspective. He turned his gaze back to the horses, and she couldn't read them at all then.

"You had to shoulder a lot of responsibility at a young

age. When most people were going out and enjoying things without much thought to anything else, you were taking on the needs of a baby and a dying friend. And then you continued right on becoming a teacher and raising a little boy that anyone would be proud to know. Trust me when I say that you stepped forward in life when others might have reacted differently." He fell silent. Laurie had felt confusion at first at the feeling of wanting to share her story with him. But now, it made sense that he would have been the one to draw her out. Because she sensed there was a lot more in common between them than before.

"I don't think we're just talking about me and my path in life. You went through a nightmare in yours…and managed to come out the other side. But it wasn't that easy, was it?"

"You see a lot. That's not something I'm used to…sharing thoughts with others."

"I'm a good listener. I don't judge because I know what it is to live in a glass house."

"As you said once before, everyone deals with tragedy and grief in their own ways. And some don't do as good a job as they would like."

Laurie had the sense that his grief was buried down deep within him to that very day. He needed to release it.

"You hide yours quite well."

"You're looking at me like you made a discovery. I'm not sure…"

"That's the persona you hide behind. You created it: a devil-may-care, shoot the rules, footloose and fancy-free cowboy, when inside you are a different man."

"I knew you might be different from other females in my acquaintance, but I truly had no idea just how different."

Laurie wasn't sure how to take that comment. "Different in a bad or crazy way, or…"

"Definitely in a really good way. And before I say anything else that might be considered *flirty*…I think we better get back. We did promise the swimming pool would be next." He stepped back and allowed her to go first. They retraced their steps to the main house. Only this time, Laurie noted that he hadn't sought out her hand. So she took a bold step without second-guessing herself. She slipped her hand around his. Their steps didn't falter, but his fingers intertwined with hers in a shared warmth of acceptance.

Chapter Nine

"I LIKE THAT little family of yours," Tori said, sidling in beside Trey on the bench under the shade tree. She nodded at the mother and son as they swam together on the far side of the pool, along with Annie and Jamie.

"They aren't *my little family*," he returned, his gaze unreadable behind the dark lenses on his eyes. "So whatever is in your crafty brain, leave it alone."

"I see."

"There's nothing to see."

"You sound like you're trying to convince yourself of that one." She continued before he could respond. "Don't get me wrong. I like them. And I can tell that you do, also. It's just that she is not the usual Trey Tremayne date material. I'm trying to figure out why that is?"

Trey's gaze fell on the woman beside him. The two of them had always had a closer relationship than with their older siblings, Thomas and Truitt. It was often uncanny how Tori knew his thoughts, and she cut right through a lot of the BS he threw up as a smokescreen to others and saw something for what it was…saw him for what *he* was. But her words were churning more feeling inside him where his thoughts were already tumbling. He shook his head.

"When you figure it out, let me in on it, too."

"Maybe you're growing up?" She said it with a teasing glint in her eye, but her tone was laced with something deeper. "Priorities change with age and wisdom I hear. Or maybe you're just shedding the stuff that doesn't matter for that which does." Then she grinned... "But, I am *not* saying anything close to you having the wisdom part. Let's get that straight. And I'll add my new diagnosis to your already long counseling bill."

"And that is the little sister I know right there." He returned the grin.

"But I also would like to add...Laurie and her little boy would be a good foundation for a good life. But only if you were truly one hundred percent in it. Laurie seems to me to be a one guy forever type of female who deserves a guy who sees her in the same way. And that means those "Rodeo Romeo" cowboy wings of yours might need a little bit of clipping. Otherwise, *none* of you need your hearts bruised up." She stood and patted him on the head. "Now I must impart my wisdom on others."

Trey watched her walk away. His gaze went back to the pair in the pool. T.J. and Andy had moved into a group of other kids and were playing a spirited game of Marco Polo. That sent his gaze searching among the other adults for Laurie. He found her seated on the edge of the pool, feet dangling in the water, as she kept an eye on the kids. *Always being mom.* Trey smiled. And he couldn't help but rise from his seat across the way and head in her direction, grabbing a cold bottle of water from the ice chest on his way.

"Is this seat taken, pretty lady?" His grin widened when she gave him a smile.

"You're in luck. Seems it's vacant right now."

"My luck, indeed." Trey dropped down beside her, handing over the cold drink to her. "I also come bearing gifts. You looked a little hot over here."

She gave him a smile and took the bottle, while her silent gaze assessed him. "You like doing that, don't you?" She didn't wait for a response. "Throwing out flirty innuendoes along with those devilish dimpled grins. I imagine that goes a long way with those buckle bunny fans of yours." She took a long sip of the water, her gaze not leaving him.

"Smart lady…calling me on it. I do slip back into 'Rodeo Romeo' now and then as my sister likes to goad me with it. But *you* are the subject right now. The girl I *do* remember found your voice, and it's a pretty nice one…unless it's being used to put me in my place."

"I'm sorry I gave that impression. But I was guilty of putting a label on you and sticking you into a neat little box. You were always meant to be in the limelight…even back in school. You're what my grandfather would call a rolling stone, always moving on to discover what's around the next bend. But seeing a bit of your life here today, you work hard at what you love to do. And that is a good thing. I can understand now that a lot of what you project is just an offshoot of that rodeo cowboy for those fans. Because I sense there's another layer under all that noise where the real Trey Tremayne hides out."

"You sure you didn't get your degree in psychoanalysis instead of teaching? You think I'm deep enough to have another layer besides what you have here next to you?"

"I saw hints of it even back in school. I admit I watched you from the back of the room. Not like those other shiny girls hanging on your every word and move...but I sensed something was there that maybe you kept hidden and I wondered what it was."

"Did you ever figure it out?"

She shook her head. "Not back then. And in the middle of my sophomore year in high school, I was moved from Faris to McKenna Springs. I think that was about the time you hit the rodeo circuit pretty heavy."

Trey nodded, his smile replaced with a thoughtful regard. "After we lost half our family, I guess I was without much of an anchor. It seemed best to put some distance behind me and see what I could do on my own. I had no idea that the others would jump into the rodeo arena in their own ways. And we joined up and decided that a united Tremayne front was what was needed. It was a good decision. It might be the best way to honor those we lost and make them proud. Or at least glad to see we haven't made a huge mess of things." He finished with a laugh.

Laurie smiled at him. He was glad to see it wasn't tinged with pity. Trey wasn't sure what emotion might be behind it. He wished he could tell. Her hair had been left down and free to dry better in the light breeze and sunshine. It glistened, and he stopped himself before he could reach out and touch its softness. He realized that something had happened to his senses since having Laurie Wilkes fall into his arms that day a few weeks back. It was strange and unsettling and had him thinking about lots of things in his life up to that point.

And for the first time in his life, he shocked himself to realize there was a slither of fear in the pit of his stomach. Laurie saw through all his BS to the person he was. She was close to ferreting out the place he hid away deep inside. It was time to get back to what he knew, what protected his feelings from those who would see too much. Tori was right. This woman beside him was different from all others. And if he stayed too long, he wouldn't ever want to leave her...and that was the push he needed to stand. "I think we need to retrieve T.J. and get packed up for the drive back to McKenna Springs. I promised to have you both home before dark."

Was that a shade of disappointment that crossed her eyes before she turned them away from him? See? He was right to put up the walls again. She and T.J. needed someone who wasn't that rolling stone in their lives. It was time to get back to where he belonged.

THE DRIVE BACK to McKenna Springs was mostly done in silence. T.J. was tired out from a full day of excitement and activity. His eyes closed not far from the ranch and stayed that way. Laurie tried to think what had precipitated the change in the man beside her. She could feel that something had changed at the pool. Had she overstepped? She could be plain spoken at times. But she wasn't a female to play games...not with people she cared about. And that was a jolt inside her that helped keep her silent on the ride. Where had that come from?

Trey Tremayne was not someone who was on her level. He never had been. She watched him in school. She could admit to having a crush on him just like all the girls who managed to capture his smiles and flirting ways. But she hadn't been one of the chosen ones. She kept to the corners and back rows, watching and dreaming. Then they had gone their separate ways. It had to be fate or bad luck that she had crashed down upon him that day in the general store. Of all people to walk in that door...it had to be Trey. *It had to be Trey.*

There were all kinds of reasons why that wasn't a good idea. A rodeo cowboy...always on the road...an admitted heartbreaker. That was not the person that she or T.J. needed to have in their lives. Even if he wanted to be there. And judging by the lukewarm temperature in the cab of the truck at the moment, that was not something she envisioned. He had done his duty…kept his promise to T.J.…had some laughs. But the rolling stone would keep on rolling…away from them. She needed to protect her heart because it was misbehaving inside her chest and was in serious danger of doing something really stupid. *Like falling for a cowboy.*

When the pickup parked in front of the general store, she didn't waste time retrieving their bag from the back seat, while Trey gently woke up a groggy T.J. The trio mounted the steps, and she unlocked the door. *Keep it short.*

"T.J., don't you have something you need to say?"

The boy's face lit up with a grin as he looked up at the tall cowboy. "I had the best time I ever had today. Thanks for taking us to your ranch and all. You're the best." He stepped forward and locked his arms around the man's waist in a move that was swift and surprised them all.

Laurie saw the shock on Trey's face and then there was a finite softening of his features and she had to have imagined the glint of moisture in his eyes before he bent his head and his hat concealed her view. His hands returned a hug around the boy's shoulders. "You are welcome, young man. It was a day I won't soon forget, either."

T.J. stepped back, still smiling. Laurie nodded. "Why don't you take the bag upstairs and get into the shower?"

"Okay, Mom. See you later, Trey." He headed inside.

Laurie felt the awkward silence. She inhaled a deep breath and fixed a smile on her face. "Thank you, Trey. You made my son very happy today. He won't soon forget this. And I won't, either. Please let your family know again how much we appreciated everything they did to make it a great day for us? It meant a lot."

"They loved having you both. You and T.J. were a hit with everyone."

Awkward silence. He cleared his throat, his hat in his hand as a hand ran through his hair. "I might not be around for a while."

And here it comes. She couldn't help but hold back a breath as she steeled herself for the inevitable. "I guess it's time for you to get back on the long rodeo road."

"Yes...I have some catching up to do. It's time I get back to working for my living." He attempted some lighthearted tones, but they were flat.

"I hope you win it all, Trey. We'll be here cheering you on with all your other fans. And we hope you stay healthy while you do it."

She sensed there was a conflict going on inside the man in front of her. Why should there be? He had said his piece and he could walk away...fancy free.

"That means a lot. Look, there's a couple of rodeo dates where we're going to be back in Texas...fairly close. The one in Dallas is a major one. I think T.J. might enjoy seeing the real thing and not just what he saw on the ranch today. I'll see you guys get some V.I.P. tickets if you want to come. If you don't, that's okay, too. No strings."

No strings. He was telling her that for a reason. She felt a ridiculous crack in the center of her chest. "Thank you. We tend to be busy in the summer given the tourists and all. But we'll see."

He slid his hat back onto his head. "Sounds good. Well, I better hit the road. Thanks for today. And...*damn.* I don't know what this is, but it is damn hard to stand here and say goodbye to you. And why I just said all of that, I have no idea. You tie a guy up in knots, Laurie Lou Wilkes."

Had the sunshine come back into the sky? What was he saying? There was a ridiculous wave of something like joy rising inside her.

"I can't say I'll be back. I can't say how I'm feeling about you...but I know I am already missing you. And that hasn't happened to me before. Take care of yourself, Laurie. And spare me a thought now and then, okay?" He lowered his head, his arms drawing her into him. His warmth filled her body and then his lips lit a torch that sent her insides up in glorious flames. Was it a goodbye kiss? Was there a hello in there? She just knew she needed to savor each moment of it as if it were both the first and the last. Because being kissed by Trey Tremayne was all and more than she had dared to dream. And then he stepped back, his breathing as deep and erratic as hers. His heated cobalt-blue gaze burned into hers.

She waited for him to speak. But he didn't. A slow smile that was tender and sad and so much more crossed his lips. Then two fingers touched the brim of his hat in a final cowboy salute and he turned and walked away. He left her standing in the same spot at the front door of the store where she had crashed into his arms...and he had stepped into her heart. Only this time, he had taken it with him as he drove away.

Chapter Ten

TWELVE CITIES, TWELVE arenas. It was a good thing Tori kept track of what day it was for him, and got him to the airports on time, and basically kept on his tail end. Maybe he came back to the arena too soon and hadn't healed or something. For whatever reason, it was harder to keep the energy and mindset on the par it used to be. He and Dace Cordero were neck and neck in the points standings. Trey used to lead by at least triple digits. He had some good rides, but he had some that should have gone better. His head needed to be in the game.

"Here's your food." Tori spoke as she entered the trailer, slamming the door of their fifth-wheel travel rig behind her. It served as Tori's living space along with their office on the road trips. Trey either bunked in one of the hallway bunk-beds or in whatever hotel he could find along the way if he had to hit a separate rodeo in order to tap out points on other broncs. He sat at the table going over the stats sheets and moved them aside as she sat the plates on the table in front of him.

"Steak, no potato, but plenty of vegetables. You need to

eat better and keep up the gym work." She said those words as she slid into a seat across from him. Her plate was a mound of salad and grilled chicken.

"I guess I should be grateful my jailer allows me to still have meat." He made the comment as he reached for the steak sauce.

"You need meat. But I'm limiting the steak to twice a week. It'll be poultry and fish the rest."

"You need to get married and boss around someone else."

She made a face at him. "You're closer to that walk down the aisle than I am. And you just remember the bet we have. I can already feel that money burning a hole in my pocket that you'll be paying me."

"Keep dreaming. Gray Dalton won't be patient forever, little sister. He'll be coming for your answer one of these days, and then you'll have to pay up as you'll be the next Tremayne down the aisle."

"I love your ability to live in a world of denial. Because I think I'm looking at a male who is fighting a losing battle. Look at me and tell me that Laurie and her son aren't on your mind at least a little every day since we've been on the road."

Trey stabbed his fork into the piece of steak and rubbed it in the sauce before he responded. "I think about a lot of different people. But I only have time to concentrate on one thing...the next ride. That's what counts." He popped the bite into his mouth.

Tori smiled at him. "I don't invest in swampland or your fairy tales. I'm just sorry you let that one get away. She might have been the right one. And who says you'll get a second chance down the road? You could grow old in that rocking chair all alone on the porch back home."

"Might be…but I'll have all your money in my pocket for being the last Tremayne standing outside the matrimonial net." He shot his grinning response right back at her.

She let it drop and he was glad of it. Her last jab about being alone on a porch was something that had crossed his mind more than once. That and a few more thoughts that left him tangled up and wide-awake staring at the ceiling over his bunk on more than a few nights. And it seemed that all thoughts eventually ended up in the same place…remembering kissing Laurie goodbye. Dallas was coming up. He dared to think about the possibility she and T.J. might show up. He had sent the tickets almost two weeks ago by special delivery. There had been no response. So she would show up or not. He had no idea what he would do if she did. Trey had a pretty good idea how he would feel if she did not come. And that was the heart of his whole problem.

"Have you seen T.J.? I thought he was getting a milkshake

and coming right back to finish up unpacking those boxes of new fishing lures in the storeroom." Laurie took the last two bottom steps quickly and headed toward the front counter where Mel stood sorting the new pricing signs.

"He left here about thirty minutes ago. He probably got sidetracked by the new display in the window of the bike shop. I hear he's saving up money to get that red one in the window," Mel chuckled.

Laurie shook her head. "That red bike...that is all I have heard about. But it's good that he wants to earn the money for it."

"That young man has a good head on his shoulders. You've done a fine job so far."

"So far," Laurie replied. "But he hasn't reached his teen years yet."

"Good luck on that one. But just take deep breaths and hang on for the wild ride. You'll make it through those, too. Of course, your hair might be all white by then."

"Thanks a bunch for that." Laurie grinned, glancing at the clock on the wall. She walked over to the large window and sent her gaze down the street, searching for a sign of her son. But there was none. She withdrew the cell phone from her pocket and hit the number for The Diner on the Square. A couple of rings and Darcy's cheery voice answered.

"Hi, it's me, Laurie. I was just checking on what might be keeping my son. He was to go and get his milkshake and come right back. Is he still sitting there?"

"Let me check around, I'm in the kitchen area. Hold on."

Laurie could hear her moving from the kitchen into the dining room. And then there was the noise of diners and clatter of dishes. "Hold on, Laurie," Darcy came back on the line. "I don't see him, but Kelly is telling me something." She was gone again.

There was a beeping on her phone at that point and another call was coming in. Laurie had a thought it might be T.J. so she could try to put Darcy on hold and switch calls, but then Darcy came online. And Laurie froze. "Hey, girl. Kelly waited on him and he got his shake but then she saw a couple was talking to him outside the window and T.J. didn't seem to look too comfortable with them. Then she got busy and when she finally managed to move over to the window again, she didn't see any of them. How about I head out from here and start walking toward your place and see if I come across him? I'm on the way."

Laurie's brain was trying to keep calm and she remembered the other call. She punched the button quickly. "T.J.? Is this you? Where are you? Answer me right now."

There was a moment of silence. "Laurie? This is Trey. What's wrong? Is something wrong with T.J.?" The calm, steady tones were unexpected and yet she gripped the phone as if it was a lifeline with the man on the other end.

"I'm probably overacting but T.J. went for a milkshake at the diner and should have been back a while ago and then he left there but they saw him talking to a couple and he didn't seem okay so Darcy is headed up the street this way looking and I am leaving the store headed her way. I really need to hang up in case he calls. Bye."

The moment she disconnected, she wished she hadn't. Perhaps he would have just stayed on the line and that would have been somehow... She saw Darcy motioning. Laurie began to run down the sidewalk to where she stood, her heart pounding with each step.

Darcy nodded her head and Laurie looked down the side street. T.J. was standing with a couple...a man and a woman. She didn't recognize them. Neither did Darcy, and *she* knew everyone. That meant they were strangers, and they were talking to her son. Except it seemed he wasn't speaking much, just nodding his head now and then. He kept moving a bit, and Laurie realized what he was doing.

She had taught him all about stranger danger when he was old enough to understand and kept it refreshed over the years. He knew he needed to keep at least an arm's length and more between him and the person he was talking to...just in case he needed to run. He would have a head start on the person pursuing him. Her protective mom mode went into high gear. Darcy was her backup.

"T.J.? You're late. What's going on?" She spoke the words to T.J., but her gaze was dead center on the couple. They were clearly surprised by her appearance. She stepped up, putting T.J. just between her and Darcy. Darcy's hands were on his shoulders.

"Who are you and what business do you have speaking with my son?" No use trying to be friendly, not when it involved her child.

"Oh my, I'm... We're so sorry. I guess we should have stopped in and introduced ourselves to you first, and we were going to do that. But we were in the diner and heard the waitress call him T.J. and then he looked so much like...well, like my dear brother and all. But I'm getting way ahead here. I'm Chloe Morgan...Chloe Morgan Jones, actually. This here is my husband, Craig. And you must be my brother's widow. I'm sorry we never got around to meeting you before now."

Laurie's brain was going through its file system a mile a minute, trying to summon forth every bit of information she could dredge up about what her husband had told her about his estranged half-sister. What she remembered made the panic level inside her go up several notches. This woman was the real reason why he sought out Laurie's help in protecting against what could happen to his son. Had he known this day would come? That the "bad penny" as he had called her for want of a nicer term had finally turned up? And for what reason?

"Yes, it's a shame that never happened. Not even at the funeral."

The woman's gaze sharpened on her. Yet, she still maintained her false smile. "We were out of the country. It would have been impossible for us to get back in time. But we're here now. Naturally, we wanted to stop in and see our nephew. He is my only living blood relative, after all. He and I are family."

Warning bells were sounding in her brain. There was a threat here. "T.J. and I have to get back to the store. I trust you all want to get back on the road before it gets later. Have a safe trip." She turned to her son and Darcy. "Let's go. Mel is wondering where we are, I'm sure."

The three of them returned down the sidewalk and then around the corner, each step Laurie expected to hear the woman's voice behind them. Yet it did not come. Could it be that easy? They made it to the store and once inside, she had to resist turning the lock and putting the closed sign on the door.

"I'm sorry, Mom. I knew I shouldn't talk to strangers, but they said they were my family and all. But I tried to come back to the store. I didn't let them get close or anything."

Laurie smiled at her son and gave him a hug, holding him against her side longer than she might normally have done. She kissed his forehead. "First, you gave me a scare. But I'm glad you remembered your stranger danger pointers. And even if they are related in some way, they are still strangers to us. Can you tell me what they talked to you about?"

"They just wanted to know where we lived and if you

had another husband or anything. What kind of work you did and why we weren't in Dallas anymore."

Laurie caught Darcy's gaze and they both seemed on the same page. "Well, there are boxes in the storeroom waiting for you. So get to it, and I am proud of you for remembering what you were taught. If you see them again, just come get me. You don't need to speak with them unless I am there with you." He nodded and headed off to earn some more money for that bike.

"Anything I can do to help out?" That came from Darcy. They hadn't known each other long, but they had developed a fast friendship. It was hard for anyone not to like and trust Darcy McKenna. "Remember, my big brother is a Texas Ranger…in case you and I need backup."

Laurie met the grin that appeared on Darcy's face along with those words. She managed to lighten the moment. But it was true. She had Davis McKenna, a captain in the Texas Rangers, on speed dial.

"I'll remember that. But I am hoping it is just my overactive imagination that is making me think that this meeting or their happening to be in Faris, is not just coincidental. Neither I nor T.J. have ever met these people before today. All these years and not a word from them. But now I know they could show up again, and I'll keep an eye out. Thanks for being here."

"No thanks needed. But you have me on speed dial, and I live over the diner so I can be here in three minutes or less.

I can also give Davis a call if you think we need to do some digging on them. Just say the word."

"I'll keep that in mind." They hugged. "Thanks again, friend."

The door opened, and Laurie was surprised to see the uniformed figure of Gray Dalton walk into the store. He was tall and the set of his jaw showed he meant business with someone. How did he know to come to their store at that moment?

"I heard there's an issue with T.J.? Has he been found? I was out in the county when I got the call. I got here as soon as I could."

"You got a call? And yes, T.J. is safe and sound and here," Laurie responded.

"Evidently you were on the line with Trey at some point, and then when he heard something was going on with T.J., he called me right away."

Trey called for help for her. That caught in her brain. Darcy spoke up in the moment. "There was a couple that had stopped T.J. and he seemed to be uncomfortable with them when we finally found them down the street. They turned out to be some relatives of Laurie's just passing through. They've moved on."

"That's a relief. I'm glad to hear that he's here and all seems to be okay. But you might want to call Trey because he might be trying to find a plane to get him here as we speak."

"I'll do that." Laurie finally found her voice. "Thank you for coming so fast and all."

"That's my job. If you need anything at any time, you keep my cell in your speed dial and don't hesitate to call me. I mean it. I'll leave you ladies now and get back to my office."

"And I am getting back to my job now, too. Talk to you later."

Darcy left and Laurie checked out the street in front of the store. She didn't see the couple but that didn't mean they weren't around. She'd just have to be on alert for the foreseeable future.

She found Trey's number in her phone log and hit redial. He answered on the second ring. There was a bunch of noise behind him.

"Are you in the airport? Please tell me that you're not in an airport. I thought Gray might be joking in some way."

"Nope…he wasn't joking. But if he found you and all sounds like it might be okay…then maybe I won't get on the plane that's waiting. Is T.J. okay? Are you okay?"

She gave him a rundown of the last hour. "And I can't thank you enough for having the presence of mind and thoughtfulness to call Gray and send him to help. My only thought was to run and find T.J. and then get him to a safe place. But it means more than I can say that you sent help like you did."

"Well, I feel bad that I wasn't there to come in person.

But Gray comes in handy sometimes."

"I thought you were riding tonight in Phoenix? At least that's what T.J. has written on the calendar here in the store's office. He seems to be tracking you." She tried to make light of the fact.

"I like that. It feels nice," Trey said, his tone lowered. "I was hoping I hadn't been forgotten."

Truth. "You haven't been." The thought hit her. "If you were supposed to ride, why would you be getting on a plane to come here? I remember what Tori said at the barbecue about how important these next rodeos were to you in the standings. You can't be missing a rodeo."

"Well, I've gotten ahead by a few points so I could take a hit if needed. And something like this, well, I... It's just good that T.J.'s okay and so are you. And you are okay, right? You won't worry yourself to death over these people, will you? It was as simple as them just stopping on their way through town?"

"Yes, that's what it was." She hoped it was, but she wasn't going to put her worry onto him. He had already done enough for them. "And you need to get going and go ride that bronc and get a lot of points. Just don't get hurt doing it."

There was a pause and then she could hear his grin even on the phone...in his voice. "Yes, ma'am. I aim to please you. I will do my best. And you give T.J. a hug tonight for me. I hope you guys get to make it to Dallas. I'll understand if you can't, but…"

"We'll be there." And she meant it.

"Then I better go get some more points. Don't worry, Laurie Lou. All will be well. Bye."

All will be well. How could he sound so sure? But she hoped with all her heart that he was.

Chapter Eleven

THE NEXT COUPLE of days were nothing out of the usual. But still Laurie couldn't shake the feeling that something wasn't right. And Laurie didn't have to wait long to see where the bad penny might show up next. Chloe Jones walked into the store just after they opened for business. Her husband was not with her. Mel was taking inventory on an aisle over from the checkout counter and Laurie was standing there as she walked up with the fake smile in place.

"Hi there again. This is quite a place you have here. Have you had it long?" The woman was looking all around at the furnishings. Laurie could almost hear the calculator click-clacking in her brain.

"It's been in the family for about twenty years or so. I thought you and your husband were passing through on your way to…?"

"Oh, yes…New Orleans. It's a fun place. Have you ever been there?"

"No. We didn't have much time to travel since Jonathan was so ill. And T.J. was so young. Then I had my job to hold on to."

The woman pretended to not hear the censure in Laurie's tones. Laurie couldn't care less. This woman did not give one thought to Jonathan and what he had gone through to try to sustain his life as long as he could. He had said she was more akin to a vulture, hovering over something in order to pick its bones for whatever she could get the easy way. And she wasn't above doing things underhandedly, either. That's why he wanted to protect T.J. And now it was up to her to do that.

Laurie waited. She didn't feel the need to make idle conversation. The woman needed to lead the way.

"I was shopping this morning, and I saw that you had a pretty steady business coming through here. You must be doing alright for yourself and T.J. You make a good living. And I also heard a bit of gossip in the diner that you're seeing a rancher who happens to be loaded, too. Not bad there for a widow. I know it must be hard to keep up with all of that and have to have someone else's kid on your hands to raise and all. T.J. isn't even your kin."

"What's your point?"

The smile faded. She looked Laurie straight in the eye. "He and I are blood kin. That counts for a lot in courts these days. I imagine it would be hard on him if he had to leave you and go live with someone else and all. But kin is kin."

"Spell it out. Why are you here?"

"Maybe it's time that I get to know my nephew. I think we'll stay around here a few days and do that."

"I don't think that's a good idea. T.J. has never set eyes on you before you accosted him at the diner. Jonathan never spoke a word to him over the years about you except to say you had left the family when you were fourteen. And only returned sporadically when you needed something." That *something* they both knew was money and she had drained his parents dry over the years trying to keep her out of trouble and away from alcohol and drugs. Of course T.J. had not been told that part of it. Jonathan had only shared it with Laurie.

"Well, I don't need anything now. My Craig does quite well in his investment business. And we're thinking of settling down in New Orleans and buying one of those lovely old plantations maybe. We're ready to have a family. And that's what married people do...but then you wouldn't know about that now, would you? You're a widowed school-teacher, trying to raise someone else's child on your own. I'm thinking there would be those educated people who might find that to be problematic and might wonder if that is the best choice for a little boy who needs a mother and a strong father figure in his life. You just never know these days."

"I think you and I have nothing more to discuss and you should leave my store. And you should also stay away from my son. I hope that is *clear* enough for you." Laurie made direct eye contact as she spoke each word. The woman was the first to blink.

"Fine. We shall see who is the smarter of the two of us."

She turned on her heel and made certain that the door slammed behind her.

Laurie stood in the same spot when Mel came around the corner. "Are you okay?"

Laurie took in a deep breath and a shaky one was let out. Her hands began to tremble a bit, but she shoved them inside the pockets of her skirt. "I don't think I'll be okay anytime soon. I just have to pray that that woman and her husband were just making a threat to see how far they could get. Maybe they'll leave and move on. In the meantime, it's just another day as far as T.J. is concerned. And he is what matters. I need to go up and take out some meat to thaw for dinner." She tried to not run up the stairs but take them sedately. Once inside the apartment though, she allowed herself to bury her face in the hands that continued to shake. What would happen next? What if they didn't go away? She had to think. She had no idea what she would do if they didn't go away. Would the law be on her side? They had married and done what they thought was right to protect T.J. Had they done enough? She just had to pray that the couple would leave, and this would be a bad dream.

"THIS IS AWESOME! We've got this whole plane to ourselves!" T.J. couldn't contain his excitement. They had arrived at the airport, following the instructions that Tori had sent to them for their travel plans to Dallas. Laurie had been shocked when they arrived at the designated gate and then had been shown through a couple more doors until they stood at the opening to a private hangar where a glistening white private jet sat waiting, the brand of the Four T Ranch on its tail. One steward had taken their luggage and stowed it, and the other had shown Laurie and T.J. onboard and gotten them settled into their seats which were deep leather-cushioned chairs situated around teak-wood tables and couches in soft tans and blues. The carpeting was thick, and Laurie was tempted to kick off her shoes and just enjoy the luxury of it. She had no idea that when Trey had said that Tori would take care of the travel arrangements, this would be what he meant.

Had she known ahead of time, she might have thanked them but turned down the travel help. On the other hand, it certainly was giving T.J. a great memory in a weekend that she hoped would do them both some good in just getting away from the strained atmosphere they were leaving behind them in Faris. Chloe hadn't approached her again since Laurie had basically kicked her out of the store. But she had been aware of them passing by the store, driving slowly and making certain they were seen. Darcy reported they had been in the diner trying to engage the waitresses in conversation involving information on T.J. and herself. Darcy had put a stop to that quickly.

Laurie knew that when they returned to Faris, she would

have to decide on what was the next best step to take. They couldn't live under the threat of this pair doing something at some time in the future. This needed to be settled. But she would deal with it next week. In the meantime, this would be a new experience for T.J. and one to make him happy. And the fact she might be seeing a certain cowboy at least for a little bit of the time, made her own pulse speed up. She was going to concentrate on the positives of the trip and leave the rest until they returned.

"This is just too cool. Trey is really a great guy." T.J. was enthralled by the view outside his window. Laurie was happy that her son was having such a great time. And she had yet something else to be grateful to the cowboy for making happen. But what would happen when, and if, that cowboy kept going down that road one day and T.J. was left heart-broken?

"Yes, he is being very good to invite us to see him ride in the rodeo. But you do know that he is going to be very busy because this is also his business...his work. And he has to travel a lot to take care of it. There could be weeks...many weeks where he might not be able to talk to you or even think about things back here in Texas. That might make you sad."

T.J. nodded his head. Then his clear gaze met hers as he turned from the window and gave his attention to her words. "I know that Trey can't stay in McKenna Springs. He has to go where the rodeos are. But that doesn't mean he won't still be my friend or yours. He likes us and cares about us, Mom. But I know I shouldn't count on him and all these fun things always being here. But it's just like you always told me. We should be grateful for the good things that come our way when they do. Some will stay with us and some won't. But always be grateful. So we can be grateful, right?"

And Laurie found she needed to take a deep breath and fight back the sudden welling of emotion inside her. Her little boy showed glimpses of being so much older than his years and having an understanding that would make any parent proud. And whatever came of things, they would be okay...bruised hearts or not.

The flight was a short one. What normally took five hours on the ground, had taken a little less than an hour in the skies. But T.J. had gotten to visit the pilots and had come away with a pair of silver wings as a memento. Once off the plane, they found Tori standing beside her truck, waiting for them.

"So did you enjoy your plane ride?" She grinned, hugging the boy who had to show off the wings first thing.

"It was so much fun! And I got to sit up front with the pilots for a little while, too. And there were video games and movies and food on the plane. It was super awesome."

"It was so unexpected, and we would have done just fine on a regular flight." Laurie smiled when it was her turn next to be greeted with a hug.

"But then my brother wouldn't have been able to have

an extra day to spend with his favorite people if you had traveled on a commercial flight that didn't have any space until tomorrow afternoon. So enough said. Let's get you all to the hotel."

They headed toward the skyscrapers of downtown and Laurie shook her head. "I had forgotten how awful the traffic can be. Amazing how one gets so used to being in a small town until you come back to the big city and are hit with all these crazy drivers. You seem to handle it just fine."

Tori shook her head. "Imagine what it's like driving through this pulling a fifth wheel rig and trailer with a couple of live animals in there, also. I've done that in New York City trying to get to the Garden a few times, and in LA. You just shut your eyes and take off."

Laurie looked at her and saw Tori was grinning. "Maybe don't shut your eyes all the way."

They pulled off the expressway and then turned into the property that looked like some fancy estate. It was the grounds that surrounded a large several-story high hotel complex on the outskirts of downtown. The valets opened doors and took the two bags very quickly. Tori stepped onto the curb.

"You are already checked in, and here are your key cards and room number. Trey will be another hour at the arena and then he'll shower and change and knock on your door at three. I was told to tell you to be ready and wear your swimsuits. Got to run. I'll see you at some point again. Call my cell if you need anything." Then she was back in her truck and pulling away.

Laurie and T.J. followed the bellman to the elevators. She looked at her son at one point and found his eyes were huge in his head as he took in their surroundings in silence. Once on the elevator, he whispered beside her. "Is this a museum or a hotel?"

The bellman smiled and winked at him. "That question comes up a lot. I guess it is both. You see the owner of the hotel is an art collector and the items she collects come from all over the world and she puts some of them on display here. So, I guess you can say it is both."

"That also means…don't touch anything," Laurie grinned at her son. Their room was on the top floor, and opening the door, the bellman allowed them to enter first. Laurie tried to remember to act not like a country bumpkin out of water, but as though she were used to such luxury all the time. *Right.* T.J. just stood in the middle of what was a living room with floor-to-ceiling windows with a view of the skyline of Dallas that was unbelievable, with his mouth open and eyes wide. The bellman shook his head when she offered him a gratuity. "It's all been taken care of for your entire stay. You have two bedrooms. The master is to the left and the guest is to the right off the main living room here. Room service is twenty-four hours and has been already taken care of, so you just sign for it. Please enjoy yourselves." And then he was gone. The moment the door closed, T.J. came alive.

"Can you believe this? This room is bigger than our entire apartment over the store."

"Well, you need to unpack and then change into your swim trunks and be ready when Trey arrives." He grabbed his bag and took off. And then she heard him exclaim again. "And there is an Xbox and games here even. Wow!"

Laurie took her bag and opened the door to the master bedroom. It was pretty incredible. It too, would eclipse the whole apartment. The draperies and luxurious bedding and furniture were too perfect to even touch in their creams and golds. She sat down in one of the chairs in front of the same floor-to-ceiling windows that covered an entire wall. Laurie suddenly felt odd and unsettled. She could well imagine what a price tag for all of this would be adding up to. The plane, the suite, and whatever else was coming. She knew the Tremaynes were well-off. They had land, cattle, oil…the big three for success in Texas. But this was definitely bumping it up a few levels. It pointed out just how wide the gulf was between the world Trey was used to and the one where she and T.J. lived. She didn't know what to think. But they were there. Just be grateful…words her son had reminded her about earlier. *Truth.* No turning back at this point.

At five minutes to three, there was a knock at the door, and T.J. barreled out of his bedroom and was at the door of the suite before Laurie could clear the door of her room.

"Hi, Trey! This is an awesome place. It's kind of like a museum, too. And the plane was the best ever."

Trey's laugh came across to her before she was able to see the man who evidently had come into the suite and was talking to her son in the foyer. "I'm really glad to see that you're having a good time so far. And I see you're ready to go swimming. You might want to get your shoes and a shirt and take them along. Is your mom ready?"

"I'm right here." She came around the corner and the breath caught in her chest. Seeing the man again brought forth a whole bunch of feelings, and she had to try to come up with a coherent thought. And it didn't help that his gaze locked on her and did not leave as she approached. She had her swimsuit on…a black figure-hugging one piece with cutouts on the sides and a deep vee in front and back…with a brightly colored coverup that was somewhat see-through but fell to just above her knees. Her hair was pinned on top of her head. His gaze said more than any words, and she felt a blush creeping up the back of her neck.

T.J. came running back with his stuff, and she had the presence of mind to add it to the small bag that had her lotion and other items inside. Her feet were in flip-flops and she saw a grin spread across his face as Trey's gaze landed on her feet.

"Nice bright red toe polish. Who would have guessed?" His gaze came back to hers.

"Something wrong with that?"

"I just had no idea until now how much red polish is my new favorite thing."

There went her breathing again. Thankfully, her son reminded them of more important things. "Are we going swimming now?"

Trey smiled at him. "Yes, that is the plan. Bet you didn't know that this hotel comes with its own private water park?"

T.J. was shocked and even more excited over that bit of news. Trey opened the door and held it for them. There were several people in the elevator so that precluded any conversation. Trey led them through the inner part of the hotel and then out onto a patio that overlooked a broad expanse of green grass and tall trees and bright flowers. And in the distance, there was the mini-water park where there were areas for small children and water slides for bigger ones and a long lazy river around it all for those who just wanted to take things easier.

"Last one in..." Trey began but hadn't finished before T.J. had tossed his shirt on a chair in one of the cabanas and he was in the water. "Guess that leaves you and me and..."

He turned to see Laurie moving past him, flip-flops and coverup left behind. "That makes you the last one." She was in the water next. She turned and smiled up at the man. He had managed to get his shirt off and that was a sight to see. The water helped keep the heat from rising too high inside her. Then the jean shorts came off and she wasn't the only female in the area enjoying the scenery. But she was the one that felt the splash when he dove in and came up with her in his arms.

"So you find it amusing? I think there's something more amusing." And she barely had time to hold her breath before he launched her in the air and let her go under in a big splash. She came up sputtering. Then the splashing battle was on as T.J. joined in...first on his mom's side and then on Trey's. Laurie gave as good as she got until she finally had to give up. She grabbed a float as it came by and drifted off into the lazy river.

"Giving up?" Trey challenged after her.

"Just a pause while I plan out my next battle move. You guys amuse yourselves. I'll be recharging my batteries."

Trey and T.J. didn't have to be told twice. Now and then she would seek them out when she came around to where they were intent on the water slides in racing each other down to the bottom or participating in a game of water volleyball and basketball with four others. She smiled seeing T.J. so happy. If only it could stay like that every day for him. But all they could hope for was the present, and she'd take it one day at a time. It was so nice to float along and let the water take her wherever it wanted. Her eyes closed and she enjoyed the drifting sensation. Imagine her surprise when she opened her eyes to find she had been secretly hijacked and had been maneuvered into a small pool where things were calmer and away from the crowded area. There were a pair of gleaming blue eyes peering at her, then a grin appeared that was definitely devilish. Trey was in control and she braced herself to be dumped into the water.

"Go ahead. Get it over with. You're going to dump me in."

He laughed. His laugh was deep-throated and made her grin in spite of herself.

"Now why would I do something like that?"

She eyed him in silent regard. "Because you're an overgrown kid who can't help himself maybe?"

"Hmmm… You might have a point there." And the next thing she knew, she was going into the water, but two strong hands grabbed her around her waist before she went all the way under. She was hauled up against his chest, and her arms went naturally around his neck to save herself. That put her in a most interesting and decidedly tricky position. He obviously could touch bottom and anchor himself. She was at a disadvantage.

"There is something to be said for acting like an overgrown kid now and then," he teased, their gazes on an even level with each other. His arms wrapped around her body and his palms were heating the flesh at her waist where the material cutouts were. It was a feeling that was heating up all sorts of things within her at the same time. There was a dark glittering in the depths of his gaze as it moved very slowly over the features of her face before settling on the lips that seemed to draw his attention.

"Do you have any idea, Laurie Lou Wilkes, how I believe I owe an apology to your grandfather's old ladder?"

"You do?" She seemed to be drawn to watching his

mouth move as he spoke with much the same intent.

"It made me realize how well you fit in my arms."

"I do?"

"You do. And there's only one other thing that is even more perfect. How your lips fit with mine." And the very small space between them disappeared.

Her heart rate shot off the charts and sparks flared against closed eyelids as her body was brought up against the hard planes of his chest, fingertips sliding beneath the material at her waist and setting fires on the flesh at her back. Her legs entwined with his, the strong thighs locking her in place. His arousal was pressed against her and a heady sensation coiled inside her at his response. It emboldened her to part her lips and invite him inside where his kiss deepened, intensifying her desire to be even closer to his fire.

His mouth moved to draw in the soft skin along the slender length of her throat and a ripple of ecstasy caused her head to slowly roll backward on her neck to invite more access to the magic touch of his lips. It was getting harder to draw in breaths. Trey lifted his mouth and then the pause allowed her to find some shred of sanity. It did the same for him. He rested his forehead against hers. "I think I proved my point about kissing. And this is not exactly the best place to begin an honest conversation like this one. But just so you know, I've thought a lot about you while on the road and I've missed you. I'm very glad you said yes and came this weekend. You *and* T.J. I hope you feel the same way."

"We're here. Whether it was wise or not, the jury is still out on that one." And she had no idea how to feel. Trey Tremayne had just opened her eyes to feelings she didn't know she could feel. But she had no idea what a man like him could possibly feel for her...a single mom who couldn't afford one-night stands with a "Rodeo Romeo" with a love 'em and leave 'em habit.

Chapter Twelve

"THIS IS SO great!" T.J. was in his element. He couldn't get over the size of the stadium, let alone the several dozen booths with all sorts of merchandise to sell, food offerings, and all things cowboys. Each time he spied one of the posters with Trey featured on it, he really became excited. "And we really know a guy on a poster and all," he explained to Laurie when he asked to buy the third poster they came upon. "Do you think Trey will sign them for me?"

"I think there is probably a really good chance of that happening, but three posters are more than enough. I think it's about time to get something to eat and then find our seats. What will it be?"

"Hey, there you two are! I couldn't get the cell phone to go through in this building, so I took a chance on finding you in this crowd." Tori appeared at their side and grinned when she saw T.J.'s purchases. "Are all those of my brother?"

He nodded. "They sure are. I'm going to ask him if he'll sign them for me, too."

"Well, if I had known you wanted posters, I have a lot of them I could have just given to you. So keep that in mind.

But I needed to see if you had eaten yet?"

Laurie shook her head. "We were just about to grab something."

"Glad I caught you. I've got food coming to my place and there's a chance Trey will drop by so I thought you might prefer to do that instead of fight the crowd in here."

Laurie and T.J. were onboard with her suggestion. They followed her through the throng of people and outside the building. She led them down a small driveway and then back to where the stock was being loaded in and out of pens. There was a lot of activity. Then they were in an area where trailers and pickups of all shapes and sizes were parked in a few rows. It didn't surprise Laurie that they stopped at one of the largest fifth wheel units on the lot, complete with a built-in horse trailer. The Four T Stock Producers branding was on all sides. Tori opened the door and allowed them to enter first.

"I'm impressed," Laurie said, her gaze traveling around the smartly furnished interior that resembled both a luxurious living room and a professional office all consolidated into one.

"This is home away from home. There's a bedroom up front. The hallway has two bunks. Bathroom, kitchen, and living area which we are standing in at the moment. And we have room for two horses or one pampered bull onboard at the back."

There was a knock on the door and Tori turned to open

it. "What are you doing?" She stepped aside after reaching for a couple of boxes from the person's hands and then the tall figure of Trey stepped through the doorway. His hands were full of white containers and a drink carrier. Tori made a space on the counter and the items were soon offloaded onto it. Then he turned to Laurie and T.J., a broad smile on his face.

"I saw the delivery guy was looking a little lost, so I asked where he needed to go, and it was here. So I saved him a trip. But you can certainly feel free to tip me for doing so." He landed that look on his sister.

"Nice try there. But I added it to the card already before he even came. Everyone gather around the table and let's eat all this while it's still warm. I hope you guys are ready for some amazing Chinese food. We get this delivered each time we're in this area. I wasn't sure what to get, so I just got a little of everything."

T.J. made certain to take the chair next to Trey. And he had to tell him all about the posters.

"I'll be happy to autograph them for you. Keep them in their tubes, and when we get back to the hotel, let me have them and I'll sign them for you. In the meantime, I'm thinking that cowboy hat is a really great look on you. Better watch out or the girls will have you in their sights."

"Yuk. I don't need any girls hanging around. But I like wearing it."

"Well, there's some hat etiquette that goes along with it,

so I'll give you some pointers later, too. In the meantime, whenever you enter someone's house or office, let's say, you always should take it off and hold it by the brim at your side. If you're staying a while, you should hang it on a hat tree or a wall peg if there's one handy for hats. If not, you set it on its crown with the brim facing up. Or sometimes I hang mine on the back of my chair if it has a spindle back. It's important to always take good care of your hat."

T.J. chuckled a bit and looked over at Laurie. She was intent on serving food onto a plate for him and then one for her. She didn't need discussion on hats to be the center of the conversation. She had not forgotten the episodes on the day she met Trey where not one, but two hats had been ruined for him. He shot her a look of amusement but wisely made no comment.

"The seats you have for the performance will put you up close to the action at the chutes," Tori said, already getting into her meal. "I'll be busy on the catwalk or behind the chutes with the pens. I keep an eye on our animals when they're loaded into the bucking chutes and then watch how they react and how the cowboy treats them."

"No cowboy dares to do anything that might upset Tori when it comes to her babies." Trey winked at his sister.

"And do I have this correct: the cowboys that rode and won the highest points yesterday will ride again tonight?" Laurie asked.

"That's right." Trey nodded, finishing up the food on his

plate. "Tonight is for the title, a fancy saddle, belt buckle and points to add to your total for Nationals…and a check, too."

"Wow, do you always get a lot of prizes when you win?" T.J. liked that part.

"Well, most of the bigger rodeos like the ones where you run up the points, give you all kinds of things like saddles and buckles, but the really big ones will usually give away a new truck sometimes."

"Have you won those things?"

"T.J.," Laurie spoke up, shaking her head. "That's not using good manners."

"It's okay," Trey said. "It's a genuine question. I can say that I've gotten my share of those things." He nodded at Tori. "And if my sister keeps racking up points with that bull of hers, she might just get a shiny truck, too…down the road."

"Well, neither of us is racking up points sitting here. It's high time I got back to work, and you, pretty cowboy, you can escort your guests to their seats and then get to work on stretches and checking rigging. You've got some serious competition tonight." Laurie fell in to helping Tori clean up the meal and soon they were outside and parting ways in different directions.

It was surprising to Laurie when halfway through the building, a family of four stopped Trey and asked for his autograph and a photo. Laurie ended up being the designat-ed photographer. Laurie watched Trey interact with the family and the young fans in his smiling, easygoing manner. And then three more patrons noticed, and a small group had formed. Trey glanced over at her and T.J. and gave an apologetic smile and shrug. A few minutes and then he smiled and thanked everyone and said he needed to get moving if he was going to meet the bronc with his name on it. They all laughed, and he left them, moving Laurie and T.J. on through the crowds. He didn't stop again.

"Here you go; looks like some good seats. Tori did come through."

Laurie had to agree. They had front row seats with a very close view of all the action. T.J. was excited and soon became mesmerized watching all the activity going on before the rodeo began.

She had a couple of minutes alone with Trey. "I'm sorry I didn't get to have breakfast with you and T.J. this morning at the hotel. Tori needed some help and with Truitt not being here this trip, I needed to fill in. It gets kinda crazy sometimes."

"I can tell. And those people who stopped you…asking for photos and autographs…is that fairly routine?"

"It can be." He seemed to be watching her more closely. "I'm sorry that you guys had to wait there and…"

"No, it's fine. I understand that's part of the job, part of being a celebrity. People want to meet you and all. And you certainly are good with them. You were very patient."

He laughed and shook his head. "Believe me, I didn't

feel patient. I was impatient to get back to you and T.J. We don't have much more time left in this weekend and then you head back to Faris and I'm off to Oklahoma City."

"Such is the life of a rodeo cowboy," she said. Laurie kept a smile on her face, but inside, she couldn't quite summon the same feeling. The Trey Tremayne that she had spent time with in Faris and on the Tremayne ranch, the one who teased and then kissed her so passionately, that man seemed very far away from the one standing in the midst of his rodeo world. And she felt the gulf widen by the minute.

"And speaking of, I need to get moving. I'll meet you two at the entrance to the arena after the rodeo performance is done. The bulls are always the last to go. Then we'll head back to the hotel and grab a late dinner. Tori has a couple of movies planned to entertain T.J. with so we can have a quiet dinner and talk...just you and me."

"Sounds like a plan," she said. "Good luck tonight. But try not to break anything important or anything else."

That slow smile and the devilish blue gleam in those eyes picked up her heart and flipped it a couple of times. As much as she tried to keep that wall in place between him and her emotions, he managed to scale it far too easily. "I think I might need a kiss for good luck." Before she could react, his fingers captured her chin, and he dropped a swift but searing kiss on her mouth. Then he was gone. Luckily, T.J. hadn't noticed. She slipped into her seat and tried to slow down the racing of her heart. Laurie knew she was in trouble. What were they doing there?

"Mom, look. There's Tori. She's waving at us." He waved back with enthusiasm. The lights dimmed and the spotlights came on, the music began, and the rodeo started with all of its spectacle and pageantry. T.J. was enthralled and Laurie had to admit it was all very exciting. T.J. kept track of everything happening with the aid of the program he begged to purchase. And naturally, there were photos and a few of them involved a certain cowboy. Laurie knew she would make certain to hang on to it and take it back home.

"He's next, Mom. The broncs are next!"

Laurie found she held her breath each time the gate flew back, and a bucking bronc spewed forth with a cowboy being tossed about like a ragdoll on its back. She had no idea how violent it appeared. The scores were very good. And T.J. pointed out that the rider that had just lasted eight seconds with a score of 89.5, was leading. Then the announcer's voice boomed out the next rider coming out of chute four would be three-time World Champion, Trey Tremayne. The audience reacted with loud applause.

Without realizing it, Laurie found herself sitting on the edge of her seat, much the same as T.J. And her gaze locked on the knot of people that were working over the chute where she could see Trey's familiar form. When the horse reared and kicked the stall gates, her heart felt like it had stopped in her chest. When the animal quieted, only then did she remember to breathe. But then she swallowed air again as there was a nod of his head and the gate swung open and the animal, a huge, dappled gray made a break for freedom. It was pounding out fury in its hooves and plunging to earth and then launching itself into the air in repeated attempts to rid itself of the man on its back.

Laurie's voice was screaming inside for the buzzer to sound, but it felt like eight seconds had turned into eight minutes. Trey was spurring, his free hand leveraging his balance in jerking movements over his head. Then the buzzer went off, and in another couple of seconds, Trey was free of the rigging and managed to drape an arm around the pickup man who maneuvered his horse next to the bucking animal. Trey was deposited on his feet to thunderous applause. The seasoned rodeo crowd knew before Laurie did that the ride was going to be scored high. The numbers came on the scoreboard...92.3.

"He did it, Mom! He won. Mom! Trey won!" T.J. was jumping up and down and shouting along with a lot of others in the stands. Laurie was just trying to get the air back inside her lungs after forgetting to breathe through what seemed an eternity. Trey was smiling at the crowd and then he was looking straight in their direction. A wide grin broke across his face, and he gave a thumbs-up to T.J. Then there was a wink for her. And Laurie Wilkes knew that the wall hadn't held very long. He had breached it easily enough. And her heart had become a traitor. The cowboy had won the evening, but he was also leaving the arena with her heart. How would she get it back?

Chapter Thirteen

"WELL, WHAT DID you think? What was more exciting…the broncs or the bulls?" Tori smiled the question with a teasing light in her eyes. She had appeared beside the railing in front of them as they were about to begin their way up the stairs to where they could exit.

"That was the best ever. Trey won but the bulls were really awesome and mean." T.J. enthused over the whole experience.

Laurie hoped to sidestep the question altogether. "Thanks so much for these great seats. We were right in the middle of all the action. This was an amazing experience for both of us."

"You are most welcome. Why don't you guys come down over here and you can walk with me across the arena and make a shortcut out of here? You won't have to fight the crowd. We'll meet up with Trey at the main gate."

T.J. didn't wait for a second invite. Laurie was quick to follow. Tori opened the gate, and they were inside the arena then. "This is an added behind-the-scenes tour." Laurie grinned.

"Complete with horse and cow patties," Tori laughed in response. "Be careful where you step."

Along the way, Tori was greeted and shook a lot of hands and received a good amount of thanks from the cowboys still around the chutes and others. Laurie noted that they seemed to have a lot of respect for her. She was evidently making a name for herself and her bulls. Maximus had once again unseated the two cowboys who dared to think they could hang on for eight seconds of terrifying hell. They went through another gate and were behind the chutes, where animals were moving from one pen to another and getting ready to be loaded for a trip back to their respective pastures until they headed to the next rodeo. A tall man walked up and needed Tori's signature on some paperwork.

"This will just take me a few minutes. If you and T.J. want to head up that ramp, it will put you where Trey should be waiting. I'll catch up."

Laurie nodded and up they went. Almost to the top, T.J. stopped. "There's a restroom over there, Mom. I really need to stop here."

She smiled. "Those two soft drinks kicking in about now. I'll be waiting right over there at the top of the ramp. You can see me when you come out."

Laurie found a place to stand out of the way of the moving bodies where she could keep an eye out for T.J. and also watch over the departing crowd for sight of Trey. As she scanned the crowd, her gaze was caught on the familiar tall form, who had come to stand with a small group a little ways from her spot. He evidently hadn't seen her yet. She was just about to wave when something stopped her. The group consisted of three females. Something kept her still and her hand down at her side.

There were two brunettes and one blonde. And it was the blonde that latched on to her gaze and held it. She was tall and curvy, and her jeans must have been painted on her. Her tank top didn't leave much to the imagination. Her jeans were tucked down into the tops of hot pink boots, and she had enough silver jewelry on her body to open a store with. And she had that sexy body plastered against Trey's. Then Laurie watched the woman stand on tiptoe and Trey bent his head. She whispered something in his ear and that trademark grin slowly spread across his face.

A rock landed in the center of Laurie's chest, and she felt the bile beginning to rise in her throat. *Tigers don't change their stripes.* That saying was being proved before her eyes. Trey had been a player in high school in more ways than one. And his charm for the ladies on the rodeo circuit was well-noted. Why did she think she was anything different to him? Why would he change just for a hometown girl?

Only her son had become involved, *not* just her. Her gaze caught sight of T.J. moving up the ramp toward her and she immediately turned and headed him off before he could see Trey. Her mind was churning along with her stomach.

"Hey, Mom, why aren't we waiting for Trey?"

"Change of plans. We need to get back to Faris tonight. So, we're going to get back to the hotel and get our things and get moving."

"Why? What's wrong that we have to go now?"

"I have to get back to the store. You can help me by hurrying now." She paused only long enough to call an Uber to meet them at the front gate. On the way to the hotel, a couple of text messages came across her phone...one from Trey and one from Tori. Then, as they exited the car at the hotel, a phone call came in from Trey. She didn't answer. Once they had their bags and were picking up their rental from the office in the hotel lobby, she sent a text to both Tori and then Trey.

Sorry, but had to hurry back to Faris due to family business. Could not wait. Have car and all is fine. Thanks for everything. Laurie and T.J.

Laurie knew she was only putting off the inevitable. Sooner or later, she would have to face the man. Or not. He was on the road for most of the next two months. She doubted he would have too much time to think about her or to miss having female company. Laurie concentrated on the road ahead of them and kept her cell turned off. She was driving and needed to concentrate on that. Laurie only looked at her phone once they had arrived back in Faris, and T.J. had collapsed onto his bed and all was quiet since it was after two in the morning.

There was one text from Tori, hoping all was okay back

at her home and to have a safe trip. And there were four more phone messages from Trey. He sounded worried. And he was concerned for her driving back so late at night. And was there anything he could do to help? And could she please call him and let him know she had made it safe and sound? She texted him instead.

Back in Faris, safe and sound. Good luck on the rest of your rides. Laurie

"IT'S BEEN ALMOST a week and you haven't spoken with her." Tori looked across the table at Trey. He had lost some ground in the standings but was still holding on to first place…by his thumbnails. She didn't add that he looked like someone who hadn't slept much in the last few days. Something had to give.

"That's right. I think we can say that she's telling me loud and clear to get lost. And I can't think what went wrong."

"Did you ask her?"

Trey gave a snort and shot her a look to match it. "Texts and phone calls. All they got me were two responses of *'all is fine… just busy with store and things.'*

"What went wrong? What did you do wrong? When was the last time you saw her?"

"I've told you. It was when I left her and T.J. at their

seats. She was smiling and we even kissed. Then I left."

"You were with her *last*, so what did you do or say?" This time he was asking her that question.

"And as *I* have said before, we walked across the arena, we started up the ramp and I had to stop and do some paperwork for Jake Mitchell. She and T.J. headed on up the ramp to meet you. End of story."

"Somewhere along in there, she had to have gotten a call or text. But why didn't I see her? Why couldn't she have waited to tell me what was going on? I was there waiting on you all to…" He stopped. And a sick feeling began to boil in his stomach. His brain pulled the curtain back on something else that he hadn't even considered.

"There is something," Tori said, narrowing her gaze across the table at him. "Spill it."

"I was waiting at the top of the ramp, maybe a couple of stalls away from it, but the people were coming and going, and then Jade Taylor stopped with her two cousins to congratulate me on the ride and all."

Tori shook her head. "Oh, geez…Jade Taylor of all people. There's the answer."

Trey was lost. "What are you talking about?"

"Well, if I was a female that was beginning a relationship with someone who had somewhat of a reputation with the ladies already…and maybe I have some trust issues if I had a child involved? Then I come along, and I see someone like Jade Taylor, the queen of the buckle bunny tribe probably being overly friendly in her usual way to a guy who just kissed me a little while before? Oh yeah, I'd probably say *'forget this drama.'*"

Trey sat there for a long moment. *It couldn't be that...could it?* He thought back to the conversation and Jade was indeed in top form, propositioning him in front of her cousins. He had laughed it off. Then she had left a lipstick imprint on his cheek and left. What if Laurie had seen all of that? Why wouldn't she have stayed and given him a chance to explain? But then...maybe she just figured he was being true to form. And Tori would be right. Laurie wouldn't give him one more minute of her time...or T.J.'s. *Damn, he had really screwed up if that was the case.*

"I've got to talk to her, but she won't talk to me. I need to see her."

Tori held up a hand. "Whoa with that thinking, mister. You walk away right now, you don't keep your head in the game, and your butt in that saddle? You will kiss Nationals goodbye this year. Where are your priorities?"

"I need to get some air." He walked out of the trailer and into the night air. He could hear the faint sound of the crowd inside the coliseum. In another hour, he would be up on his next ride. And Tori was right. He needed his head in the game. But for the first time, there was something else involved in the equation. It was his heart. He had always scoffed and made light of when each of his brothers had met their "demise" and fallen to cupid's arrow. How had it happened? When?

But they should have warned him. So he could have seen some clue of what was headed his way. And he had just stepped in a deep pile of horse manure with Laurie. She wasn't a game player. She had laid the cards on the table right up front. This wasn't a world she was used to being around. And she hadn't met a lot of the married and settled rodeo cowboys and their families...some of whom traveled right along with them in fancy rigs that were home away from home for the entire family. There were things he should have shown sooner to her. But he thought there would be time. He had planned a late dinner for the two of them and some serious discussion. But none of that had happened. Because he had been stupid.

Trey was between a rock and a hard place for certain. His heart told him he should be on the next plane out to find Laurie and make her understand...and make as many apologies as needed for a second chance. *Beg* if need be. But his head held his feet planted in Oklahoma soil. Because if he left, he would probably fall behind in the standings. And that would mean a very good chance of a losing season. And that would be letting down his family. They had all put their lives and many other things on hold for the good of the family business, and each person was critical to that success. What could he do? What should he do? How did one balance that with what was in his heart that he wanted to do? Each came with a loss.

LAURIE HAD BEEN back in Faris for just over a week when trouble walked into the door of the general store once again. Her heart was still bruised from the trip to Dallas and blocking Trey from their lives. So she was in no mood for Chloe to show up with her husband Craig in tow. Mel kept her eye out for T.J. who was due back from visiting a friend and taking in a movie. Laurie drew them into her office and shut the door.

"I won't ask you to sit because I'm busy and there's nothing to say." Laurie had lost all patience with the couple.

"Well, your little trip to meet up with your boyfriend in Dallas doesn't seem to have left you in a very good mood," Chloe said, with a smile that was more of a sneer. "Things not going well with lover boy?"

"Best be… That's a lot of gravy train to miss out on." Those were the first real words she had heard Craig speak. "He and that family of his are loaded and then some."

Laurie had a sinking feeling begin in the pit of her stomach. She didn't care for where they might be headed in their thinking. "My personal life is no business of yours. Why are you still hanging around?"

"Because we like it here. And we have an appointment with an attorney tomorrow. And then another one with child welfare. I don't think things like rendezvousing with a rodeo cowboy and taking along a poor, impressionable child is quite the thing to do if you claim to be such a good parent. Jonathan wasn't in his right mind when he married you...you probably had something to do with that. All those drugs he was on. And surely not in any condition to sign documents where little T.J. was concerned."

"You are out of your mind," Laurie seethed in response. Her hands doubled into fists at her side. How dare the woman bring such vile lies and innuendoes into their lives. She felt fear, also. But she couldn't let that take over. "No judge is going to listen to someone with such a long history of drug abuse. Jonathan's main concern was keeping his son safe and away from *you*."

"Now, now, ladies, calm down some," Craig spoke up. "Every problem has a solution. I'm sure you want to keep T.J. And he wants to stay here. After all, he'll have so much once you and that cowboy tie the knot. So much you probably won't know what to do with all of it." Then he smiled.

Laurie saw it all. They thought Trey Tremayne was their meal ticket and the two of them could benefit from such a proposition. They had no idea that Trey was out of their lives. What a mess. But she needed to buy time. "I wouldn't think about messing with the Tremayne family. They own this part of the state. And now, you need to get out of this office and never set foot anywhere near my son or me again. Get out."

Chloe wasn't going to go, but the man grabbed her wrist

and motioned his head toward the door. "I'm sure once you and your boyfriend have a discussion, we can come up with some good terms. We'll be in touch soon." They left.

"Those two give me the creeps," Mel said as Laurie moved slowly toward the front door. "I hope they won't be back."

"I need some fresh air. I'm taking a walk."

Laurie moved down the sidewalk, not really with a destination in mind. She wanted to scream. She wanted to run and hide. But neither of those things could she do. So she just continued to walk until she ended up on a bench in the shade of the courthouse square. It was late afternoon, and most people had left the downtown area for home. She sat in silence, watching the shadows of the leaves on the branches above her as the fading sunlight caught them.

"You look deep in thought. Solved the world's problems yet?" The voice was deep and yet tinged with friendly questioning.

Laurie looked up and met the smile of the sheriff. Gray Dalton removed the hat from his head and looked around the quiet grounds. "Guess you didn't come here for a game of checkers either. Mind if I sit?"

She shook her head and attempted to return a smile that wasn't her best. "The world is on its own I'm afraid. And I am a lousy checkers player."

"I've never been one for small talk. But when I see a pretty lady who is generally seen with a happy smile on her face around town and moving a mile a minute, I might be worried when I see her sitting alone looking like the weight of the world is on her shoulders. So given the fact I am one to want to help the citizens of this town whenever I can, I think you might need a sounding board. I'm a good listener...or so I've heard." The grin was infectious. Laurie felt herself respond.

"You remember that couple that stopped T.J. and were talking to him that day?"

"Yes, I do. The same couple I've seen driving around town a few times and going into your store earlier today when I was across the street."

"That's them. And to keep a long story short, they threatened to take me to court to take T.J. away from me, bring in child welfare. Or...I could just pay them off." She saw the look on his face that had lost its grin.

"I think you might need to fill in the details for me. Then we'll put our thinking caps on."

Laurie told him everything. About Jonathan and his concern about who would care for his infant son, their marriage of convenience to protect T.J., how they managed over the ensuing years, and then how Jonathan's half-sister had shown up looking for a payday. And since they had heard she was seeing a Tremayne, they had assumed they could cash in on that, too.

"So," Gray began after a minute of silence had passed when Laurie completed filling in the details. "They came here to blackmail you and extort money. Interesting."

"Is there anything that can be done to stop them? Do they have any legal right to T.J.? I can't afford some expensive lawyer to fight them. And I certainly can't bribe them to go away. Aren't you sorry you sat down here today?" She tried to lighten the moment but there just wasn't any way to do that.

"I can see all of that. And that is why I'm going to give this some thought and we'll come up with something. I can guarantee that. So now you can share that load on those shoulders. Those two people made a very bad mistake by coming into my county. I'll walk you back to your front door, and then I've got some work to do." They stood.

Laurie shook her head. "I have no idea what you are thinking about, but I trust you when you say that they made a bad mistake in coming here. I guess I just let things get me down recently. I usually am a fighter. But I do feel the load has lightened a bit. Thanks to you."

He smiled and nodded, placing his hat back on his head. "Two heads are always better than one. And we all need to take a deep breath now and then and let someone else take the reins for a mile or two. So find your smile, Laurie Wilkes. I think I see a little boy standing on the sidewalk waiting for his mom in front of the store."

Laurie looked ahead and saw T.J. wave at them. His grin was bright and carefree. And she was determined to keep it that way.

Chapter Fourteen

TREY HAD GOTTEN into the truck and slouched down in his seat, his gaze looking out the window beside him, but not really noting anything of the passing city. In two days, they would be in Utah. And even farther away from Texas...away from Laurie. He was more torn as each day had progressed. He should be on a plane headed south, not in a truck headed...to the airport. He sat up and then looked over at his sister.

"Did we change our plans? I don't think there's room on the plane for the horses. Or are they going to drive themselves to Utah and you and I are flying there?"

Tori shook her head. "There's a change of plans, you got that part right. But only half of the rest. *I'm* driving the horses to Utah. And *you're* getting on the plane. But you aren't headed to Utah. You are taking a detour to the south...to Texas. Laurie and T.J. need you. But you don't know that because she'd never tell you."

He was lost. "Sometimes you don't make much sense so let's back up a bit. *You* are the one who said I had to make a decision and get my head back in the game. Now, you're putting me on a plane. What happened to Utah? And pushing the points higher? And what would Laurie not tell me? She isn't telling me anything because she isn't talking to me."

"She isn't talking to you, but Gray did some talking to *me* last night. And once you get on the plane, you can talk to him and he'll fill you in. As for points, you can skip Utah and still remain even. But you have to be back for Wyoming. So that gives you four days to help out Laurie, and then get back into the hunt again. Got it?" She pulled up in front of the terminal, putting the truck in park. "But I have a question and it requires a simple yes or no."

Trey nodded. "Shoot."

"Are you in love with Laurie?"

There was no hesitation as he met her gaze dead-on. "Yes."

"Then don't just sit there. Move it." She put the truck's gear back into drive. Her eyes on the road ahead.

Trey slid out of the truck but turned back. He wasn't going to mention he had caught the glimmer of something that looked awfully like a tear or two before she kept her gaze averted. "I'll give Gray your love while I'm at it." He shut the door just in time as her foot hit the gas.

"HERE'S YOUR SUIT that Aunt Sal had ready for me to pick

up. She's been filled in and will take care of the rest of the group at the ranch. Mel's got T.J. on a trip to Austin with her grandson to see a bunch of historical stuff and then spend a couple of days at her daughter's house on the lake. Your investigator faxed the last of the reports to my office an hour ago and Calla Rose is looking at all the paperwork and will be ready with her arsenal should we need her. Her husband, the county judge, knows what might be expected of him, and is also on standby. And there's the restroom where you can change. You have ten minutes." Gray took a breath and then smiled.

Trey felt like he had been taken inside a twister, spun around a few times, and then spit back out in Faris. His head was spinning with all the details that had transpired in such a short time. But Gray was right, there wasn't much time. He had to hope that Laurie wouldn't be even madder that he would be walking in the door without her knowing about it beforehand.

He went into the restroom dressed as a rodeo cowboy. He came out less than ten minutes later, dressed in a western-cut gray suit, white dress shirt, burgundy tie, his best gray Stetson, and a quick shine on his boots. The sheriff nodded. "Better than Superman. Let's hope you can be the superhero today."

Trey climbed into the sheriff's SUV, his heart beginning to pound much the same as before he sat down on the back of one of his bucking broncs. "Who is the judge? What do you know about him?"

"It's not a *him*. Her name is Judge Miranda Morales. She's new to the bench. But she's thoughtful and runs a tight courtroom. She follows the letter of the law. I think Calla Rose once worked with her in San Antonio in a law firm there."

"And she agreed to see that pair of lowlifes in chambers?"

"Since a child was involved, she made the exception for an informal meeting of all parties. I think it was a nod to Calla's request."

"Laurie has no idea what we're doing?"

"She knows that I've gotten an investigative report on the pair. That was thanks to an old Army buddy of mine who partners with his brothers in one of the best investigative firms in the country located down in Houston. We do favors for each other now and then. He left no stone unturned. That should be enough in itself. Then we have Calla there in case anything is needed along legal advice lines. And then there is the ace in the hole...*you*."

"Ace in the hole," Trey repeated. "I've never been called that before." The courthouse came into view. and he felt his stomach give a twist. "Laurie may not be pleased."

Gray looked at the man who came to stand beside him, eyes on the tall, imposing structure ahead of them...where Laurie would be waiting. "I can't say I know how you feel right now. But I think Laurie will do whatever she needs to do for her son. And if you're part of her achieving his safety, then I think she won't want to take your head off...at least not right away." He winked and they began their walk.

LAURIE STOOD IN the conference room, pacing and pausing and then pacing some more. She finally stopped beside one of the large windows that overlooked the downtown street with its early afternoon traffic and people coming and going along the sidewalks taking care of business or shopping. Everything seemed perfectly normal. *Normal.* What she wouldn't give for it to be just a normal day. How had life turned upside down so quickly? A week ago, she was planning a weekend in Dallas with Trey, and there went the pain in her stomach again. It had to be all the stress and no sleep. And the thought of a man that she had no idea how she was going to put out of her mind...or heart.

But she had kept those thoughts shoved away due to the issue at hand with Chloe and Craig and their legal threats. And now she stood in a courthouse, dressed in her navy suit, with a cream blouse and navy high heels. Her "funeral" outfit is what T.J. often kidded her with. Then she realized that he was right. Each time she had to attend a funeral or some such solemn event, she wore this same outfit. Her stomach churned, and the dizziness that she felt earlier managed to be stilled.

In the background, she could hear Calla speaking on the

phone to her husband. They were such a nice couple, and she had turned out to be the older sister of Lily, the woman they had met when Trey had taken her to lunch a couple of weeks ago. It seemed like a year ago now. So much had happened. She wished she had the man beside her now. And that was a silly thought. She was used to facing life head-on and on her own. Laurie heard a chair scrape the floor. Calla must be finished with her call. Then a door opened and there was some murmuring. The time was coming for them to go in and see the judge. She had to be strong. She was on her own and she had to dig deep to remember how far they had come, she and T.J. They had fought battles before. But none as important as this one.

The room was silent and that cut into her thoughts. Had Calla left? She turned and then she stopped. Her eyes had to be playing tricks. Her thoughts had to be clouding her vision. Because that could not be Trey standing beside the table in front of her, his hands tucked inside the pants' pockets of an expensive suit, the jacket unbuttoned, and his gaze fixed on her. He could have stepped out of the pages of a men's fashion magazine. And he looked so very good. Her heart cracked even more.

"Hello, Laurie. I hope you don't mind that I'm here today. But Gray filled me in, and it seems I'm deemed the 'ace in the hole' whatever that might mean."

He sounded even better than he looked. Part of her should tell him to leave. But then part of her was screaming for him to stay. She had to say something. "I'm not aware of what he means by that, but so far, he has been a godsend. He and so many others. I'm just sorry that for whatever reason you had to be pulled into this." She stopped and then another thought struck her.

"Why *are* you here? How can you be here? You're supposed to be with Tori and getting points and winning and..."

"Tori put me on the plane this morning and told me I had up to five days before I was to be in Wyoming or else. I didn't question her. I ran for the plane. Gray met me at the airport when we landed with my suit and here I am. I have a short amount of time to tell you the next part of the plan according to Gray and Calla." He left his spot and moved to stand within an arm's length of her. Laurie's heart was reacting without her permission. Her pulse rate kicked up and she tried to maintain her breathing. But looking up into his blue gaze, she felt herself drowning. When he reached out and took her hand, there was no fight in her. The warmth of his palm was a soothing balm to her system.

"Before we go in, I need to give you something. It's borrowed from Aunt Sal. She sent it along with my suit. The idea that they have that we're a couple and the fact you did spend the weekend with me in Dallas, has taken on a life of its own and they mentioned it to the judge. She may have some questions. To that end, I agree with the others that you and I become an engaged couple...for the time being. And as such, you need to wear this."

He reached inside his pocket with his free hand and brought out a ring that caught the light in the room and shot it back in sparks. It was a square-cut diamond solitaire set in a band of smaller diamonds. It had to be at least two carats in the solitaire alone. It took her breath away. He slipped it onto her finger while she was still in shock. It fit as if it had been made for her...a fact that surprised them both.

"I think one of us needs to say that this is a sign." His words were more serious than anything else even if he had tried to make light of the moment. "It seems to have been made for you to wear."

"I'm shocked. That you're here. And you have placed an engagement ring on my hand, and we are supposed to pretend that we care about each other? Will that fool any-one?"

"Whether people believe us or not is up to you and me. It's for T.J. I think that can motivate anyone to do anything. I know that I intend to do my best to make people believe it. And I know that you and I need to set aside the issues we still need to talk about until all of this is settled. But I do want you to know that I am not leaving Faris until we do have that talk. So how about it? Laurie Lou and Trey...at last."

How easy it would be to say yes...a real yes to it all. If he had asked a real question. But it was make-believe, and Laurie Lou Wilkes knew how that particular dream would end. It had ended many times in her daydreams all those years ago in school when she drew her initials and his into silly hearts on paper that no one ever saw. But it was reality time. And it was very serious.

"It'll be a short engagement if you call me Laurie Lou again."

He grinned that grin that cut the deep grooves beside a mouth that she remembered so well. And there was a gleam in the eyes that looked at her with something very close to wanting, and was he leaning closer? Would he kiss her? Would she let him?

"We're ready, you two." Gray stuck his head in the door. "All set?"

They both put smiles on and turned to face him. She raised her hand and the ring finger showed off its new adornment. "Quite a surprise in that plan of yours."

He had the good grace to look a little sheepish. "A fellow has to hedge all bets. Let me be the first to congratulate you two." He turned and left them to follow before she could find something like the stapler to launch at him.

"I AGREED TO hear this informal discussion with all the parties involved as a courtesy because there is a minor involved. It is always best not to subject any child to a court proceeding unless absolutely necessary. I like to think we grown-ups can step up and act accordingly to find what is in the best interest of the child." The judge took control of the meeting and laid the ground rules in a frank and swift manner.

They felt they would be in good hands. He noted Laurie sat still, and he could feel the small tremors going through her as he still held on to her hand. He wished for the hundredth time that he could have spared her all of this. And he tried to not look in the direction of the pair sitting across from them as he would want to do something that the judge would throw him in jail for and toss away the key. But it would make him feel a whole lot better.

"Look, Judge, we can..." Craig spoke up, but he didn't get far.

"Mr. Stanley," she said, looking at the attorney that had showed up with the pair. "You would do well to keep your clients quiet until and unless I speak to them and ask a direct question. Is that clear?"

"Yes, Your Honor." He whispered something to Craig that did not make the man happy. But he kept quiet.

"I have read the papers submitted to me. Mrs. Jones, you were the half-sister of Jonathan Morgan, correct?"

"Yes, Your Honor. He was my last living adult relative and..."

"Yes, will suffice. How often did you and your half-brother visit in the year prior to his death?"

"Well," the woman glanced at her husband who was no

help, "we traveled a bit so I can't say that we were able to see each other in that year."

"In the three years before he died, how many times?"

"We were out of the country a lot. And we were all so busy."

The judge simply sat and looked at the woman until she squirmed under the intense look.

"None, Your Honor."

"So when the child was born, you did not visit?"

"No, ma'am."

"And until you came across him here in Faris three weeks ago, you had never seen nor spoken to him?"

"That wasn't our fault, Your Honor. It's…"

"My client is sorry he spoke out." The attorney looked at the man.

"No, we haven't been able to see him." Chloe spoke up at that time.

"Mrs. Morgan, you and your husband were married when T.J. was three?"

"Yes, Your Honor."

"You have been the sole support and the sole parent to him for the last five years?"

"Yes, Your Honor."

"Jonathan Morgan made provisions for his son and his son's future. Could you explain those and why he chose to do it in such a fashion?"

"Jonathan knew he was dying from cancer. He was very

concerned about who would care for his son and who he wanted in his life and who he did not."

"Who did he not want? Please provide any information on that decision as you can."

"He was most emphatic that his half-sister Chloe does not have any involvement with T.J. He had explained to me early on that he considered her to be a bad influence due to her drug history, her history of stealing, and doing other things for money that were not legal, and generally associating with people who did drugs and worse. He made me promise that I would see to that and carry out his wishes. He knew I would keep T.J. safe."

"Your Honor, if…" Their attorney began to speak, but the judge's palm silenced him.

"How long were you two married before his death?"

"We were married for less than a year…a little over six months. We had known each other for over two years prior to that. We were next door neighbors, and I would often babysit for T.J. when his dad had to work extra shifts."

"And in all this time, you never met or saw or heard in any way from Chloe and Craig Jones until they arrived in Faris?"

"No, Your Honor. I did call the number we had for her when Jonathan died. But the woman who answered said she hadn't been around for several weeks and had no idea where she could be. I left word with the woman in case she returned to please call me as I had news about her half-brother.

I never received a call."

"Mrs. Jones, why is it that you wish to take this child away from the woman who has been his mother for most of his life and who is, according to written documents, the woman designated to care for T.J. until he comes of age?"

"Because he is my only living blood relation. She isn't related to him. She didn't give birth to him. She lives in an apartment above a store. She has no husband. T.J. needs a male role model in his life. He needs two parents. My brother was under the influence of drugs when he wrote all of that shit...*stuff*, I mean. Sorry, Judge. But a single woman who flies off to be with her lover and takes along a kid... What kind of role model is that?"

"Mrs. Monroe, what are these drugs she has mentioned?"

"Jonathan was in a lot of pain in the final months and weeks. But he told the doctor to withhold the painkillers for three weeks. He wanted to have a clear mind, have the doctor verify that. Then he signed the paperwork in front of a notary, and it was filed. He did this because he wanted there to be no excuse levied on his physical or mental capability in making sound decisions. He endured a great deal of pain in order to safeguard this for his son's future. I believe you have been supplied with the affidavits from those doctors on this subject."

"What do you do for a living, Mrs. Monroe? Where do you live?"

"I am a teacher, Your Honor, in Dallas. T.J. and I live in

the same apartment that we shared with his father before he died. We are staying for the summer in Faris, taking care of the general store owned by my grandfather while he is honeymooning in Florida. He is also helping his new wife pack up her home in that state and moving her to Texas. We will leave at the end of summer and return to our home in Dallas, where I will move up to teaching third grade."

"What is this trip that has been brought to my attention?" Trey squeezed Laurie's hand lightly.

"Might I make a statement at this point, Your Honor?"

"And you are?"

"My name is Trey Tremayne. Laurie and her son, T.J. came to Dallas as my guests to watch me participate in a rodeo being held there. They had never seen such a professional event before. They stayed as guests of my family's company, in the hotel owned by my aunt. It was also a trip I had planned for a much more special reason. It was during this trip that I asked Laurie to be my wife and she said yes. Only my family and closest friends were aware of this. We had planned to announce this when I returned from the rodeo circuit in a couple of weeks. But with the advent of this meeting, I felt I needed to fly in to be here with my fiancée."

"I see. So you will be part of T.J.'s life. Are you prepared to take on such a responsibility...being a rodeo cowboy?"

"I love that little boy, Your Honor. His mother has raised him to be a fine young man. It's an honor that Laurie and T.J. have taken me into their lives. I feel it will be a privilege to have the responsibility and take it very seriously."

"May I add something, Your Honor?" Calla spoke up, handing the judge some papers and copies to the other attorney. "I felt it would be advantageous to the court to know that being a rodeo cowboy is a simple term at best. As a three-time World Champion Bronc Rider, a spokesperson for numerous major brands, and part owner in the Four T Land and Cattle Company, a local ranching entity begun in 1832, here in this county at its heart, plus a controlling interest in the Four T Rodeo Stock Producing business, he has several avenues of income at his disposal. You have been provided his profit and loss statements for the last five years. He is a businessman and a rancher who also participates in the pro rodeo circuit."

The judge took a few moments to scan over the numbers. Her expression did not change. But the other attorney and his clients' features were close to shock. It was apparent they might have just *thought* they knew he had money. But they did not have any idea just how much there was behind this *cowboy*.

"Mr. Jones, what is it that you do?"

"Well, Your Honor...I invest for people. Different things such as land, real estate, that sort of thing."

"Where is your office?"

"I believe in being fluid. We aren't tied to any one spot. I'm more accessible to my clients by being able to go to them and to check on the investments in person and all."

"Your Honor, I believe I can help shed some light on Mr. Jones and his various investments and businesses." Calla asked for permission.

"Very well. I prefer details."

"And I would like to ask the local sheriff to step in and provide additional information that he has graciously gathered for your information."

"Very well."

"Your Honor, I don't see…" The opposing attorney spoke up.

"I do see. I want all the facts pertaining to this matter." She shut the other attorney down very quickly.

Gray came in, and he handed the judge a folder. They waited as she read over the pages. Then she looked up.

"Thank you, Sheriff Dalton. I assume that there is someone else waiting outside?"

"Yes, Your Honor."

"I thank all of you for being here today. However, I must state that I am not one who takes the wasting of my time lightly. It is very clear to this court what is going on here. Fact…Mrs. Jones did not care enough to visit, call, text, or in any way contact her half-brother during the years leading up to his death. She did not see fit to make contact with his widow or his son, for eight years after the child was born. Laurie Wilkes was married to Jonathan Morgan in a legal ceremony recognized by the state of Texas. She was for all intents and purposes the only mother this child has ever known. She has provided, through hard work and dedication, for his every need and will continue to do so. I believe that T.J. will also benefit from the upcoming marriage of Laurie Monroe to Trey Tremayne, an upstanding member of this community.

"It is clear to me that any attempt to contact Mrs. Monroe or her son T.J. will be against the wishes of this court. But that will be the least of your worries, Mr. and Mrs. Jones. The papers that the sheriff has placed before me are warrants for Mr. Jones from the states of Nevada and California. They frown on bad check writing, fraud of real estate, blackmail, theft of property over $25,000 and the list goes on. You will be taken into custody, Mr. Jones, by the sheriff and remanded into his custody. As for you, Mrs. Jones, you have wasted the court's time with this frivolous and groundless legal wrangling. I am a smart woman, and I can easily put two and two together and ascertain what your true motives are for being here today. This matter is now done. Sheriff, discharge your legal duties pertaining to Mr. Jones. Good day."

Laurie, her heart pounding in her ears, stood up as Trey was shaking the judge's hand. Calla turned to smile at her and then that is the last thing Laurie remembered. Everything went black as she slipped to the floor.

Chapter Fifteen

"SHE'S GOING TO be okay. You should go home and clean up and you can come right back. We're here with her."

Laurie couldn't place the voice... It was female, and it was familiar. But then it faded out. She needed to open her eyes, but the lids would not move.

The next voice that filtered through the fog was Trey's. It sounded upset. He was angry. Then he sounded sad. The words didn't make sense, but she could feel them. She needed to leave her soft, warm place in the darkness and push through to open her eyes.

Then a sliver of light came through. Another voice came with it. A man, and he was speaking to someone else. "Dehydration, anemia, lack of sleep...a perfect storm building until there had to be a release and her body shut down. Don't worry... She'll be back on her feet once she gets some rest and we rehydrate her."

Her eyelids were able to move. Laurie slowly opened them, her gaze taking in the fact that wherever she was, it was dark, a single light burning from a lamp across the room.

It wasn't very bright. There was an empty chair. Then there were machines that had squiggly lines and lights beeping on and off. And then there was a hand next to hers. And that hand was part of an arm, that lay across her waist. Then she realized that the soft place had turned out to be a chest…a chest that belonged to a familiar cowboy. His large frame was balanced on the edge of a bed, a hospital bed and she had curled herself up against him.

Or had he gathered her against him? Whatever it was, it made her feel protected and safe and so she stayed still, feeling the rise and fall of the chest beneath her cheek, the beating of his heart matching her own. It was a place she could stay for a very long time. But then memories began to filter in. She remembered the courthouse and the meeting. She remembered how it had all ended with her passing out. And now she was in a hospital bed and Trey was beside her, still clothed in his suit sans jacket. There was stubble along his jawline, so some time had to have passed. How much? And where was T.J.? Who was taking care of him? That made her move a bit and he sensed it. Eyes flew open and the blue washed over her. A smile moved slowly over his lips and then up into his eyes as he looked back at her.

"Sleeping Beauty wakes. It's about time." The words were whispered.

"Where am I and why? Where's T.J.? What day is it?"

"And she's back," he said, not moving away. It seemed neither of them was willing to move from the warm cocoon encapsulating them. "First of all, T.J. is okay. He's still with Mel. All he knows is that he gets some extra fun time with friends at the lake. You passed out at the courthouse because of stress, dehydration, and anemia. A perfect storm took you down. But the doctors are taking good care of you, and your body is coming back to a good place again. And you had a nice sleep so that helped. You came in on Friday at noon, and it's now Saturday night. You will probably get to go home tomorrow afternoon if the doctor says okay. Except you won't be going straight home. Aunt Sal issued the order and you're going to the ranch for a couple of days until you get your strength back."

"I have to take care of the store."

"And she figured you would worry about that, so she and Annie are handling those duties since the Gallery is just around the corner. Darcy is also joining in with them. Mel will be back on Wednesday and taking over. Everything is planned out and nothing for you to do but rest. No more worries for you. Craig Jones is on his way to Nevada. Chloe is still in town but not for long. She leaves on Tuesday bound for the East Coast. Seems she's planning her divorce."

"And you've been here the whole time as evidenced by your clothing and that beard you've got working there."

"Guilty. I just wanted to be here when Sleeping Beauty finally woke up. And all it took was a few kisses and a whole lot of watching you lay here and breathe. But it was worth it."

"You kissed me while I was out? That's being rather presumptuous."

"Hopeful…bold…grateful. I'll allow I am guilty of all those. And you need to rest now."

"I will as long as you leave and go get some sleep yourself. Deal?"

"If that is what you want, then I'll do it. So I can clean up and get back here to see what the doctor has to say on his next round." He moved slowly and her warm cocoon was gone. He picked up his jacket, tie, and hat from the chair, and then he stepped back to her side. "Dream about me." Then he bent and placed a gentle kiss on her forehead. It melted her heart. She watched him until the door closed behind him.

Trey had stayed beside her the whole time. He could have left. He could have returned to the rodeo circuit. But he had stayed. He'd held her as she slept, and he had kissed her. A prince had kissed a sleeping beauty and she had woken up. But that story had a happy ending. How would theirs end?

"I HATE TO be such an imposition. I tried to get Trey to take me to my apartment, but he is stubborn."

"And Trey is standing right here," he responded, tongue in cheek, as he set her bag at the foot of the bed in one of the guestrooms in the main ranch house.

"You did your good deed and now Laurie needs to settle in and rest a bit. Doc Robbins was most emphatic about her not overdoing anything right away. I had Trey bring up a small refrigerator for the dressing area. There are bottled waters and juices in there right now. If there is anything else we can put in there for you, snacks or fruit or whatever, you let Trey know and he'll handle it."

Laurie shook her head and settled on the edge of the bed. "You all have been so kind. The last thing I wanted was to be a burden."

"Nonsense," Aunt Sal responded. "We take care of each other in these parts. Your body needs rest to recover its strength. There is nothing for you to worry about at the store. All of that is covered. T.J., as you heard when you spoke to him on the phone on the way out here, is having a ball with Mel's family. That leaves nothing for you to do but relax and allow Trey to wait on you hand and foot." She finished with a grin at her nephew. "Now, we are *both* leaving you to rest. I put you here on the bottom floor so you wouldn't have any unnecessary stairs to climb. Later you can get some walking in after your nap. Let's go, Trey." She left the room ahead of him, giving them a moment on purpose. But it would only be a moment.

"We've got our orders. I'm glad you saw things my way. I'm leaving now." He was teasing her, and if she had a bit more energy, she might have launched a pillow at his retreating back. He paused at the door and looked back at her. "I'll be grilling steaks tonight on the patio. Rest up and bring your appetite." Then he was gone.

Laurie leaned back against the pillows, enjoying the feel of the soft comforter, intending to just close her eyes for a moment. That moment lasted for two hours.

"Don't put a steak on for me," Aunt Sal said, as Trey walked into the kitchen a few minutes later. "I'll grab something in town after the Gallery closes. I have a chamber of commerce meeting tonight, so I won't be home until after nine probably. Thomas and Jamie will be at the meeting also. Pops and Dottie have babysitting duty tonight, so he'll be around over at their place if you need anything. Did you hear from Tori today?"

Trey nodded. He checked on the covered tray with the marinating steaks on it. Then he slid it back into the refrigerator. "They're leaving Utah in the morning. Truitt should pull in with the fresh stock trailers about the same time she makes it to Wyoming."

"That's good. Now I know I don't need to tell you, but...I will anyway. Just remember that Laurie needs to be careful and let her body mend. Make sure she does just that." The words were accompanied by one of her no-nonsense looks. They reminded him of the looks he often was the recipient of from his mom.

"I hear you loud and clear."

"You know I want all my kids to be happy in their lives. And I try not to interfere. But you flying home like you did, and then standing up and being there for Laurie with the judge…well, I just want to say that I'm awfully proud of what you did. And it has me thinking that you just might care for her and her son more than you want to let on. Am I right?" She matched his blue gaze with her own.

"Yes, ma'am…you'd be hitting the nail on the head. But I'm not too sure how she feels about such things with me. She might not think a rodeo cowboy is exactly what she had in mind as good husband material."

Aunt Sal placed her hand in the center of his chest. "There's a mighty big heart beating inside you. It's always been that way for all the bravado you like to hide behind. And if Laurie is half as smart a young woman as I think she is, then she already has a pretty good idea what you're made of. So I take it that you'll be hanging onto that ring for a while longer…just in case?"

He smiled and nodded. "I thought I might."

She went up on tiptoe and placed a kiss on his cheek. "I'm proud of you. And I'll be rooting for you." Then she left him standing alone in the kitchen. He had a feeling he might need a whole lot of people rooting for him. The clock was ticking, and he would need to be leaving soon to get back to the circuit. But he needed to have a serious discussion with Laurie before he left.

All he knew for sure was that he never wanted to go through again what he did when he turned from speaking to the judge to see Laurie simply close her eyes and crumple toward the floor beside him. It was pure instinct that allowed his arms to shoot out and catch her before she totally hit the floor. He gathered her up in his arms and then Gray and his deputy had been moving them fast down the stairs and into a waiting SUV. It would be a lot faster than calling for an ambulance and then waiting and then heading to the hospital that was just a couple of miles from the center of the town.

Trey kept calling her name and begging her to open her eyes as he cradled her against his chest. They were waiting for them with a gurney as the SUV sped into the emergency area. Then she had been taken away by a cluster of medical personnel and he was left to pace the hallway. All he knew was that he didn't want to ever feel that helpless again.

He ran upstairs, stripped, and then stepped into the shower. A quick shave and he pulled on fresh jeans and a royal-blue shirt. He rolled up the long sleeves and tucked in the tails. His hair was combed into place and would finish drying while he got the grill heated for the steaks. Back downstairs, he paused outside the door to the guestroom where he hoped Laurie was asleep. He glanced at his watch. He'd give her another half hour before he woke her so she could get ready for dinner.

It was setting up to be an awesome Texas sunset over the

distant hills. Shadows were lengthening across the pastures and soon the white-tail deer would move out to taste the sweet grasses. He decided that it was too nice not to set a table on the patio and eat outside. Trey hoped it would please Laurie. Baked potatoes went into the oven. Fresh broccoli was steamed. A salad was fast. And then the steaks went onto the grill. He heard a door slide open and to his surprise, Laurie made her slow way across the stone patio. Trey pulled out a chair for her, but she hesitated.

"I'd like to stand for a little while. Maybe walk a little around the patio and get my legs to stop feeling like rubber. But I *will* take a glass of that iced tea you have on the table."

"Your wish is my command." He poured her a glass and handed it over. She had evidently risen earlier and showered and freshened up. The sundress with its spaghetti straps was a soft spring green with little rosebuds in yellow sprinkled across it. It showed off softly tanned shoulders and a very nice length of legs. Sandals left those red painted toenails exposed, and Trey had to stifle a smile as he turned to check on the steaks and turn them over.

"It smells very good. I hope I can do it justice."

"Well, red meat is on the menu per the doctor's list, and we have a lot of it walking around on our land. Might as well take advantage of that fact." He grinned at her and took a sip of his tea as he walked along beside her. It was a companionable silence, yet not.

"Your aunt is such a nice lady. She and Jamie and Darcy...the way they offered to help out with the store. And your aunt opening her house to me. There are a lot of good people in Faris. I had forgotten that about small towns. I guess I've been in the big city too long."

"Maybe you have." He nodded. "Have you ever considered coming back here...or some other small town and teaching?" He hoped he didn't sound like he was fishing, except that he was.

"If you had asked me that six months ago, I would have said no. But being back here, and meeting so many of the people who have made both T.J. and me feel like we're really part of them already... Well, it's something I hadn't expected."

They walked a little farther and she stopped. They were next to a stone bench that had been cut into the rock wall. Trey noted the slight tremor in the hand holding the tea glass to her lips.

"Why don't you take a seat here and let me get some more tea for us and check the steaks, too." He reached for her glass and she agreed.

"Good idea."

He left her to enjoy the view as it overlooked the sloping lawn that filtered into a small creek separating the area of the main house from a pasture of rolling green grass and dots of black cattle grazing here and there.

"Here you go," Trey said, making a quick trip to return with teas and a food report. "And the steaks are looking good."

"Thanks. And they are smelling great. I think my appetite is waking up."

"Good. We'll get some good food in you and you can enjoy some of this fresh country air and sunshine, and you'll be back to yourself in nothing flat."

"Yes, Doctor Tremayne," she couldn't help responding, a small hint of smile on her face.

"Okay, make fun. But your real doctor is right. And I'm going to do my best to see you follow his plan as long as I'm here."

"You do have to leave soon," she reminded him. "You can't win very many gold buckles sitting on your patio with an invalid."

Trey gave her a long look. "You aren't an invalid. And sitting here on this patio with you or anywhere else, has become a lot more important than adding buckles that just gather dust in a display case."

That brought her attention and gaze up to meet his. It was time to get to the heart of the matter of the boulder sitting square in the middle of the road between them. He turned to face her more squarely. He'd take her hand. but he wasn't sure that would be a welcome move at the moment.

"Look, I'm not one for speeches or making small talk… I think you know that by now. But there's something that we need to talk about and get out of the way. I'm thinking that you left Dallas like you did, because you might have seen something that you didn't have the full story on. And I want to bring that out and lay it on the table."

She didn't try to change the subject. In fact, she gave a small nod. "I'm listening."

Tori was right. He hoped he could articulate what he needed her to know and understand.

"Jade Taylor. I'm thinking that you saw me talking to a group of ladies. One of them was Jade Taylor. She is hard to miss in any group because of the obvious way she flaunts her attributes to every male in the vicinity. If you thought that she and I were more than friends, then you'd have been wrong. I will admit that a few years ago, when I didn't have much sense, we had a one-night stand. But that was it. When she found that I was my usual uninterested self, she and her cousins moved on. That left me standing and waiting and then worrying like crazy as to where you and T.J. might have gone.

"But that really brings up a bigger subject that we need to get out of the way." He stopped for a moment and gathered his thoughts. "I've never been one to explain my actions to very many people. Actually, I guess my parents and my aunt are the ones I could count on one hand. But they mattered and their opinions of me mattered more than most. And now, I want to explain some things to you. Because *you* matter.

"I didn't handle the death of my parents and sibling, even Skyler...very well. In fact, I ran from dealing with it. I left home basically the day after graduation and never looked back. I hit the circuit as a snot-nosed kid. I thought I knew it all. And after a while, after winning some of the bigger competitions, and playing along with the media, I began being the footloose and fancy free, love'em and leave'em 'Rodeo Romeo' that they tagged me with. Why not? What did it hurt?

"But after a while, it became really old. People were using me, and I was using them. And I didn't like that version of me. And thankfully, I had my siblings here and Aunt Sal who brought me down to earth with some hard thuds along the way. And then, I was literally nailed to the ground one day by this spitfire female that somehow made me want to be a better me. Only I don't know if I can be good enough. Because I think you and T.J. deserve someone who should be a lot better than me in your lives. And that's a long ramble but I hope it made some kind of sense."

Was she ever going to say anything in response? Laurie had fixed him with that solemn "teacher's" gaze that made him want to spill his guts.

"Thank you for spilling your guts as you put it. I do know how difficult it is for most people to put their personal thoughts out there sometimes to others. And the fact that you included me in the small group that you felt comfortable doing so with, well that is something I would never take lightly. I think I can understand a lot of things better. I remember hearing how it seemed you couldn't wait to shake the dust of Faris from your boots the moment graduation was over. I wondered if it might have had something to do with losing our family earlier that year. I also thought that the Trey Tremayne that I observed in high school, was a lot deeper than the shallow celebrity-type I heard about off and on over the years. Then again, what did I know about rodeo and that life? But I know that the man I've gotten to know again over the last couple of months, is not the one portrayed on the posters and in gossip rags. And I need to admit that although I might have begun to see that I also felt insecure because there is such a vast difference in our two worlds. Maybe you did prefer girls like that Jade person…and I certainly could never compete with someone like her. And I wouldn't want to do so. So I left you in Dallas, and I was wrong to ignore your calls and treat you the way I did. I should have stayed and met it head-on. I'm sorry."

Trey did finally reach for her hand. She didn't pull it away. That had to be a positive. And her words did give him a lot of room for hope. "I think I'd like to hear more of what you have to say on the subject."

"Well, I think the first thing I would say, is that I think we should table this discussion until after our dinner because I see flames."

The words took a moment to sink in, but then he shot a look over his shoulder and he swore under his breath and took off. He opened the grill and found smoke and some flames where the grease had sparked. Grabbing a fork, he quickly removed the meat to a platter.

Laurie walked up at the same time. She looked at the main course of their dinner. Then she grinned. "I did say that I like my steak well-done. Good job, chef. It looks perfect."

Chapter Sixteen

"I PROMISE THAT I do know how to cook a better steak. I will make it up to you."

Laurie had to laugh. "For the umpteenth time, I really do like my meat well-done and this steak was just like I like it cooked. And it is very hard to go out and have my steak actually cooked the way I like it even when I tell the waitress to tell the cook he has permission to burn it. So please, you can see that I ate every bite of it. And all of the rest of the things on my plate, too. The meal was excellent and the company even better. I am already feeling a lot better."

That brought forth the slow grin that matched the light in the deep blue gaze that shared their warmth with her each time she had looked over at her dinner companion. "Then I'll take it that my prescription for this evening might just be as good as your doctor's?"

"Better. But watch out…you might need to get a bigger hat if you let that go to your head."

It felt good to share laughter with the man across from her. She felt better for many reasons but they all seemed to have something to do with Trey. He had spoken from the heart earlier and laid out some personal things that she knew had been hard for him. But he had made the effort.

"It makes me happy just to hear you laugh. That sounds strange, I guess. But it's the best way I can describe how I feel." Had he embarrassed himself? Because he stood up and began gathering their plates and glasses. She stood also.

"I've got this. You're a…"

"Don't even finish that sentence, cowboy. I think I am capable of carrying empty plates and bowls into the kitchen. I'm not an invalid." She left him to follow.

Working together, the chore of cleaning up went very quickly. He had one more surprise for her. Opening the refrigerator, he took out a dish. Turning toward her, he opened the lid. "And I waited to see if you ate all your dinner or not, so I do have a reward for you. If you have any room left."

"That is *not* Darcy's homemade cherry cobbler from the Diner on the Square is it? You've been holding that out all this time?" She was already reaching for a fork from the drawer beside her. She reached for the bowl, but he evaded her hand.

"I don't know. I might need to hear another compliment on the cooking tonight. And a proper thank you might go a long way."

"Oh, is that how it's going to be?" She met his teasing with her own. "And just what might constitute a proper thank you besides my saying again how wonderful it was, and I do thank you for all your hard work."

"Hmm," he considered the situation. "What would a bowl of cherry cobbler be worth, I wonder?"

"How about a kiss?"

Now that earned her one of his sexiest, full-blown smiles and it tickled all the way to her toes. She crossed the space between them and went up on tiptoe. He leaned down to meet her halfway. And then she quickly placed a smack on his cheek, not his mouth and grabbed the bowl from his hand that was caught off-guard. The mouthful of cobbler disappeared, and she gave him a big grin as she turned on her heel and headed toward the den. "I'll share if you ask nicely but get your own fork."

Side by side, on the couch, Laurie did share the dessert. When she had finished off the last bite, he set the bowl on the table beside them. His arm slid along the back of the couch as somehow the space between them seemed to have disappeared. His gaze narrowed on her. "What's that I see? Some cherry cobbler left behind?"

Laurie looked at him with a question raising her eyebrows. Trey leaned over and his lips went to the corner of her mouth, his tongue flicking out and capturing a small bit of cobbler. He didn't move too far away.

"I think that was the best bite of the whole bowl. Must have something to do with it being in just the right spot." His breath warmed her cheek and she was helpless to move away. When his lips returned, this time to run the tip of his tongue lightly over her bottom lip, she couldn't help parting her lips and inviting him inside. Of one accord, their bodies melted together, her arms moving to wrap around his neck and draw him as close as possible.

Trey's hands moved to her waist and slid around to draw her down onto the couch. His body stretched itself alongside of hers, his kiss diving deep within and drawing a response from within her. She had been like a person thirsting in the desert for the feel and taste of him again.

"Oh, Laurie, you do drive me crazy, girl." The words were whispered hotly against the skin of her throat. A soft moan escaped her and that brought his lips back to hers. Then he stilled, not a movement, not a sound. Had she done something wrong? Before she could voice her question, a finger went against her mouth. And then she heard the sound of footsteps moving across the kitchen floor, the sound of the dining room door swinging shut. And she froze.

Her gaze was locked on Trey's as they lay face to face, side by side. And Laurie knew a swift stab of embarrassment at the situation. Trey sensed her discomfort. That's when she watched a slow smile smooth across his mouth. For whatever reason, he was finding something amusing about the situation. Neither of them moved.

The footsteps were at the door of the den, but they did not come into the room. Then Laurie heard them turn to leave, and she felt a sense of relief coming. But then they stopped. A familiar voice came across the room loud and clear.

"Trey, you forgot to turn on the dishwasher. And it's time that our patient got some rest. See you in the morning." Then the footsteps faded down the hall and up the stairs beyond.

Trey began to chuckle. That galvanized Laurie. She pushed the finger away from her mouth and then with a push of her knee, Trey ended up on the floor. Laurie scrambled up from the couch, arranging her clothing and wishing the floor would swallow her up. They had been caught like a couple of teenagers necking in the living room.

"Hey, what's the rush?" Trey had lost the chuckling, but still retained the grin as he pushed himself up off the floor.

"How embarrassing! What is your aunt thinking right now? She knew we were on the couch. There's no telling what she thinks we were doing in here." She paused to take a breath before she added in her whispered voice. "And what is so funny about this?"

"She's upstairs in her bedroom. Why are you still whispering? And we are two adults, not kids."

"Exactly! We should have known better. I'm a guest here in her house and…"

Trey's arms drew her into them. His thumb caught her chin. "And she won't make a big deal out of it. She's a pretty cool lady. And she knows how I feel about you, so lighten up, Laurie Lou. But she's right. I should be a gentleman and walk you to your door. So you can dream some sweet dreams about me. *Or*...you can dream about what we might have done if she hadn't come home early." That made a very warm blush creep up her neck.

"I'll leave the fantasies to you. I'll do better to dream about cherry cobbler." She didn't wait for him to walk her anywhere. Let him think about that!

THE NEXT AFTERNOON, T.J. came bounding down the stairs from the store's apartment. His grin was a mile wide when he saw Trey. "Are we really going fishing?"

Trey grinned at the enthusiasm. "I don't usually stand around with two fishing rods in my hands. Guess that means I'm waiting to find a good fishing partner. Would that be you?"

"It sure is! Is Mom going?"

"No, I am not...not this time. I have work today. But I will have a nice dinner on the table when you guys come back with the fish you catch. How does that sound?" His mom came around the counter and gave him a quick hug.

"How about you go out back and pick us some really lucky worms to take along? Maybe Old Sourpuss will be hungry today and come check out what we have."

"Sure thing!" T.J. was off in a hurry.

"And please try to stay on the bank and out of the river this time?" Laurie gave Trey a joking reminder of the first time they had gone fishing, and all three of them ended up in the water and the fish on the bank. He had the good graces to look a bit sheepish.

"Well, I might have had a distraction or two that day. A certain female who kept needing her hook baited."

"I got them, Trey! Some really big fat ones." T.J. came back with his treasure box in hand. Laurie shot an amused smile at Trey.

"And that's that... So you guys have fun and be safe." She placed a swift kiss on her son's head as he headed toward the door that Trey held open for him to go ahead of him. The cowboy sent a slow wink in her direction. Then he followed after his fishing partner.

"You're certainly looking much better today." Mel had exited the office and caught the last of the pair leaving. She had a knowing smile on her face as she looked at Laurie. "Those cheeks have a rosy glow on them. Couldn't be because of a certain Trey Tremayne, now could it?"

Laurie just gave another smile. "I've got to get the paperwork caught up today, so I'll be buried behind my desk for a while."

Laurie could feel the warmth in her cheeks, and it matched the warmth in the rest of her body since coming down the stairs earlier and finding Trey standing at the bottom, that incredibly sexy smile on his face, and his gaze fixed on her. She had held on to the railing to make certain she wouldn't do something silly and stumble. The even sillier thing was that he had dropped her off at the store earlier that morning after bringing her into town from the ranch. So just a few hours later, he came back into the store with fishing rods and asked permission to take T.J. fishing. The fact that he wanted to do that and had remembered how much it meant to T.J. the first time, it totally touched her heart.

The truth was loud and clear between her head and her heart. As much as she might have tried to deny it over the past few weeks, Trey had strolled right in and refused to let go of it. They came from such different worlds. He was a single rodeo cowboy who lived his life on the move. She was a single mom, a schoolteacher, who needed to keep a stable world for her son. He came from wealth and a close-knit family who were upstanding members of the community. She had no family left but for her grandfather who was a storekeeper in his general store.

But for all the reasons why a relationship would never work for them, there were other reasons why she couldn't walk away. *The heart wants what it wants.* That saying kept floating through her mind on more than one occasion since coming into the orbit of Trey Tremayne. Perhaps it had known what was ahead of them even back in their high school days? This was always meant to be?

Laurie just knew that the man who stood up beside her and had been there to protect her and T.J. when Chloe and Craig had dropped into their lives, the man who made her laugh and opened her heart to the possibilities of finding the person wanting to share her life, who took time to care when she fell and hurt her foot and who was beside her in the hospital when she woke up, and he was the man who took time to make a child happy by taking him fishing…that was one and all wrapped up into one person. *Trey.*

The dark cloud over the day was the fact that the clock was ticking. He had his life and responsibilities to get back to tomorrow. And she knew her heart would break to see him go. But she couldn't ask him to stay. And she knew that even if she could, she wouldn't. He had his dreams. And she understood about those. What could a future look like for them? And the most important questions: Did he even want a future with them? Or would tomorrow be goodbye for good?

Chapter Seventeen

"YOUR CASTING IS getting more natural, T.J. Have you been practicing?" Trey had watched the boy bait his hook, carefully following Trey's instructions and a wide smile lighting his face when he achieved it and then placed the line back into the water.

"Yes, sir. I put one of those little lead weights on the end so it would be like a worm sort of…and then I went out back of the store and just kept trying to get better. Just in case I got to go fishing again."

Trey nodded. *Smart kid.* "That's being resourceful. And it's paid off for you. Keep working at this and Old Sourpuss won't stand a chance one of these days." That brought another smile from the child, but he also saw it faded almost as quickly as it had come.

"Is there something on your mind?"

There was a shrug of shoulders. Trey waited a couple more minutes, standing silent and keeping his eyes on his line that was a few feet away from T.J.'s.

"It's just…well, Old Sourpuss might get caught before I get to come back and go fishing again. My mom and me, we'll be leaving in couple of weeks, when Gramps gets back. I won't get to go fishing in Dallas. And we probably won't come back here until a whole year...not until next summer. People will forget us even."

Trey knew about the fear of losing people you cared about...no matter the circumstance. And he didn't want T.J. to have to deal with that feeling of fear and rejection and loss. It was like a ball of twine with lots of different layers and hard to separate if too many knots were allowed to stay for too long. That's the analogy he had used to describe the feeling he found too often in the pit of his stomach when he was both searching for something and running away from the loss of his family.

But that path, in spite of the twists and turns, had taught him a few things along the way. He was stronger and tougher than he thought. He could own his decisions. And family was the most important thing to him. Let people think they knew the bronc rider with the devil-may-care smile and attitude. It didn't matter to him. Until the day Laurie Wilkes fell into his arms. And maybe the final bit of sense was knocked into his head. That elusive arrow that he had watched take down both of his older brothers had snuck up and caught him totally unawares. That elusive thing called love. No planning, no preparation, no fighting it. One moment your brain wakes up and your heart knows. The next steps were up to him. Trey knew that he had big decisions to make. But he also knew that his decisions were probably already made if he was honest with himself. And that included being honest with both Laurie and T.J.

"Do you like living here better than living in Dallas? What about your friends there?"

"I have friends here…Andy, Jamie, and there's Mel, and Darcy. And you."

Trey felt a pull in his chest at the way the boy said the last words. "What about your mom? Think she likes it here better than living in the big city?"

T.J. nodded. "I think so. There's not a whole bunch of traffic and the people she said really have time to be friendly and get to know you. She smiles more now than when we lived in the city. And I think she's happy here, too."

Trey knew he needed to bring up another subject with the child. "You know, I have to leave tomorrow. I need to get back to the rodeo circuit. It's going to be a pretty busy time for me. But we can keep in touch by phone calls and emails and such. If that's okay with you? And then you can let me know how you and your mom are doing?"

Another shrug came. "I guess so." Then Trey was surprised when T.J. drew the line out of the water and set his rod and reel beside the cypress tree beside him. He drew in a deep breath as if he had made up his mind about something. He turned to Trey, his arms folded across his chest. Trey set his rod and reel to the side and stood prepared to listen to whatever was on T.J.'s mind.

"Seems you have something weighing on you. Something

I can help you with?"

T.J. looked up at him with those clear green yes. "Can we have a talk? Like man to man even though I might be a kid?"

Trey had no idea how to tread through this possible mine fiend, except to take one step at a time and be truthful. He nodded. "Do you like my mom? Like could she be like your girlfriend maybe?"

"I do like her. I like her more than a lot. I don't know that she likes me the same. That's something only she can say right now. How do you feel about me saying I like her?"

"I think it would be awesome if you and Mom liked each other. Then maybe we could even stay and not go back to Dallas. But my mom needs someone really good to take care of things and be around and be like a real family and all. I heard you say at the rodeo that you liked being on the road and traveling. Guess you couldn't do that if you had someone like a kid hanging around and all."

Trey folded his arms across his chest much the same as the boy had his. He gave some serious consideration to what was just said. "You know, T.J., your mom deserves a lot. I agree with you. And yes, I am on the road a lot. But you didn't get to meet a lot of the people that rodeo around me. If you had, then you would have met many of them that have their families traveling with them...especially in the summertime. And there are some that homeschool their children as they travel year around. So there are all sorts of people in different situations and many who have families along with them. But that would be something that would have to be discussed and agreed upon as to what would be best for say, you and your mom." He went down, resting on his haunches to be able to look the child more fully eye to eye. "There's one thing I want you to know. I consider you and your mom to be a dynamic duo…you come together, not separate. That's how I see you. *You* are just as special to me. I can't say what will happen down the road, but just remember I want you and your mom to be happy. And I appreciate that you and I could have this talk. You're quite a young man. Are we good here?"

That earned a smile from T.J. and a nod. Trey held back the urge to give the boy a hug and opted for a handshake. The boy put his palm in his and they made a gentlemen's agreement. He stood. "You know I hate to say this, but we're going to have to let your mom know that we might not be bringing home the main course tonight. I better call her. How about you gather up the things and we'll pack up?"

Trey withdrew his phone and Laurie answered on the third ring.

"Don't tell me," she said. "Which one of you fell in?"

He smiled. "We are both dry. But sorry to disappoint you about counting on fish for the main course tonight."

Her soft laugh floated across the phone and the smile went from his face to his toes and back again. "I haven't begun the food yet, so I'll look in the freezer for a substitute."

"I have a better idea. How about we swing by the Pizza Palace and load up on some carbs? I'm watching T.J. nod his head like a bobblehead doll in agreement with that idea."

"Then who am I to pass up a chance not to cook?"

"I need to make a couple of stops in town. I'll drop off T.J. so he can get some of the riverbank off him, then be back to pick you both up at six."

"Sounds like a plan."

THEY COULD HAVE been any other small family hitting the local pizza restaurant after a day's work. The Pizza Palace was doing a steady business, both dine in and take out. They had chosen a booth along one of the sides of the room. Sounds of laughter and pings and blasts came from the adjoining room that served as an arcade with various games inside. They placed their order for two medium pizzas, one a supreme and one just pepperoni per T.J.'s vote. Sodas came with it, along with a salad.

"Do I have to finish the whole pizza before I can go and play some games?" T.J. had kept an eye on the comings and goings in the adjacent room. He had made sure to mention that he had some of his summer savings in his pocket just in case.

"If you finish your salad, and at least three slices, I think that might be a deal," Laurie said, smiling across the table where she sat sharing the booth beside Trey and her son sat across from them.

"Deal," T.J. nodded, his concentration on his plate now.

Laurie had freshened up before Trey arrived. She chose a blue denim skirt from the closet and a soft yellow top with frilly cap sleeves to wear with it. Yellow sandals showed off freshly painted toes. Her hair was loose to fall around her shoulders and down her back. She had wanted to make the effort because she also knew that this would be the last time Trey would be with them before he left. And then she tried to not think about anything else to do with that subject. She was determined to enjoy every moment and worry later about what was to come tomorrow.

Evidently, Trey had made a quick stop off at home also and showered, which showed when he arrived by the slightly damp hairs along his collar and ears. The dark blue, long-sleeved shirt only heightened the blue of his eyes. She noted how female gazes couldn't help but follow their trio as they crossed the room to their booth. That pleased her in one way, but also pointed up another fact she didn't want to think about. Trey would be going back to the circuit where predatory females like Jade Taylor and others would be lying in wait. *Leave it for tomorrow.*

And Trey seemed to sense some of her thoughts. His warm palm closed over hers as it lay between them on the leather seat. A light squeeze brought the realization that he was there with them at that moment and that might be a memory for tomorrow, but it was reality at that minute. She'd hang on to that.

"Now did I forget to write something on my calendar? How could I forget pizza night with such a nice group of people?" The voice belonged to Sheriff Gray Dalton, who had come up and was leaning one elbow on the back of the booth on T.J.'s side, a grin on his face.

"Yes, amazing how that happened." Trey responded with a smiling shake of his head.

Laurie smiled. "Please, do join us now. There is more than enough here."

"That is mighty tempting, but I just stopped by to pick up a to-go order that I'm taking back to the office. I need to burn some late-night oil on staff evaluations and budgets. So no rest for this public servant. And no time to enjoy such good company. But I'll take a rain check."

"No rest for the wicked," Trey said, shaking his head in mock sympathy. "I'll be sure to mention to Tori when I see her tomorrow, how busy you're keeping. Any message?"

Laurie noted the change in the gray eyes. And the stiffening of his body as he pushed out of his leaning casual stance. The hat was slid down on his head. "I doubt she'd be interested in any message. But you have a safe trip. Rodeo is a demanding mistress." He touched the brim of his hat in her direction, gave T.J. a pat on his shoulder and then he walked away to the front register. He picked up his food and left without looking back again.

"Guess things aren't going well right now between him and my sister," Trey observed. "But it'll pass. Gray's an easygoing guy."

"He's a very nice guy," Laurie responded. "I hope your sister knows how lucky she is to have someone like him who obviously cares so much about her."

"I'm done, Mom," T.J. piped up. "Can I go to the game room now?"

"Yes, you may. Thanks for finishing the rest of your food. We'll come get you when we're ready."

"I'm sorry about not being able to bring home the bacon," Trey said with a chuckle. "I mean…the fish. They just nibbled and that was it. Old Sourpuss lives for another day. But T.J. and I won't give up. We'll get him yet."

"You'll have to do that on your own," Laurie replied. "T.J. and I leave for Dallas soon. Back to our regular lives. And a rodeo star doesn't have much time for fishing, does one?"

Trey grew quiet for a moment. His hand tightened around hers. She looked at him and waited. Something was coming and she almost didn't dare breathe for the dread weighing on her chest in those moments.

"I've never been less ready to get back on the circuit. Since Dallas, it's felt different for me. It's hard to explain. But I know that you and T.J. coming into my life has caused me to think about things in a whole new light. I think going back may help that become even more clear in my mind. At least, I'm hoping that. I need a clear head to do my job or some bronc might rearrange my thinking for me." His comment was meant to elicit a reciprocal smile from her. Laurie tried to do her best. But her brain wasn't in the mood for laughter.

The last thing she wanted was to be the reason Trey might not have his mind in the game on each ride. He needed to go back to the rodeo head whole...and heart whole. She also knew she couldn't be the reason he gave up his dreams and then might end up regretting his choice. *Set him free...if it's meant to be...* She didn't allow herself to finish that thought. Laurie had a fairly good idea how it would end up.

"You belong in that rodeo arena. It's who you are. You wouldn't be happy any place else...not for long. You are a bright and shining star. You always were. Even in school, I knew you weren't meant for the lives of people like the rest of us humans. T.J. and I will always applaud you from the sidelines. No one will be bigger fans. And T.J. will have something really great to boast about with his friends back in Dallas...where we belong. Where life makes sense for us."

She stood. Because she was about to lose it from the pain of her heart imploding inside her chest. The look in those blue eyes were almost her undoing. He was so con-fused...and when the twist of pain began to shadow them, she couldn't stay and watch. "It's time I get T.J. We need to get home. I've still got a lot of paperwork to catch up on before Granddad gets back next week." She left him sitting alone and did not look back.

TREY WENT THROUGH the movements expected on the outside. He managed to laugh at a corny joke T.J. shared on the way back to the store in the truck. And answered a question about something to do with rodeo that he couldn't recall much about later. Laurie sat in the passenger seat and kept quiet, her gaze finding something interesting outside her window.

On the inside, that was a different case. Questions were firing through his brain a mile a minute. He was questioning every moment, every conversation, even every kiss they had shared over the past several weeks. Had he gotten things so wrong? He didn't think so. Perhaps Laurie had just decided that she wanted no part of a rodeo cowboy after all. And that twisted the knife in his gut even more. Trey never apologized for his choices in life. He had never questioned them until Laurie had come into his life. Maybe he needed to get back to where he belonged. Maybe then he would have some perspective. Maybe then, he could find his old self again. Only would he still want to know the old self? And how long would it take to forget what he was leaving behind?

Chapter Eighteen

"HE IS RIDING like a mad man." Truitt made the comment as he stood above the chutes having just watched Trey's latest ride on a bronc called Skull Crusher. His exit was a flip over the hind quarters of the thrashing animal much to the crowd's delight. Then he swept his hat off his head and gave a bow to the crowd that only made them get louder in their approval.

"Yes, he is," Tori agreed. "The press and the crowds are eating him alive. And he's hell bent to live up to the hype. The flip side of that, is that it's put him way ahead in the points. Unless something unforeseen happens, he's headed for Vegas. If he doesn't break his neck first."

Truitt shook his head. "Someone needs to kick some sense into that brain of his before a bronc does it."

Tori looked over at her brother with a sarcastic smile. "Why do you think I had you come meet us here? Because I missed your sunny personality so much?"

"That figures." Truitt turned toward the steps and Tori followed. "You have any idea what this has to do with? What changed?"

"Laurie Wilkes is what changed." Tori didn't hesitate in her response. Truitt turned at the bottom and she stopped beside him.

"I thought that was over before it began? Didn't she go back to Dallas?"

"Yes, she did. But I don't think it was ever *over*...for either of them. I think he's trying to get 'over it' in all the wrong ways and that includes riding like he doesn't have any caution. It makes for a great show, but the odds are stacking against him. I'm sure hoping you can stop him..." And that's when her voice faltered, and Truitt realized that he had never seen his sister on the verge of something remotely close to tears. That both touched him and angered him. His gaze softened on her.

"I'll give it my best shot, little sister."

Truitt found Trey signing autographs at the outside door of the arena. He had been stopped by a half-dozen fans...five of whom were female. Trey kept smiling, fending off their less than subtle offers of fun after the rodeo. He looked up and saw his brother and he made short work of the admiration party. He walked over and shook his brother's hand.

"If you can tear yourself away from your adoring fans, I think Mama Josephine's is still open outside the grounds. We can grab some of those enchiladas and tamales."

Trey nodded. "So that's what brought you all the way from Texas to Colorado? I knew it couldn't be missing me or Tori."

Truitt turned without responding. They jumped into Truitt's truck and headed away from the crowds. A few minutes later, they had a table in a quiet corner of the back of the small restaurant, the jukebox stuck on playing every George Strait song ever known. Trey noted the autographed photos on the walls as they entered...mostly of George and a handful of other lesser stars. There was even a smattering of rodeo cowboy posters up there. Trey didn't miss how his brother raised his eyebrows at him when he noted the fact that there wasn't one touting Trey Tremayne.

"Must not be fans," came the taunt as they placed their food orders and then were served their drinks. Truitt took a deep draw of his beer, then got down to business.

"Since when did you stop riding broncs and start putting on a clown act for the fans?"

Trey finished the gulp of drink he had just taken and then met the gaze narrowed on him from across the table. "So you didn't just come for the food? You came to give me a critique on my riding? Last time I looked, I was number one in the standings. Isn't that where I should be?"

"What I just saw was an act. It wasn't a skilled rider going head-to-head with a great mount. What gives? And don't try to bullshit me... That meter is still working just fine where you're concerned."

"That's what I like about you, Truitt. You do get to the heart of the matter."

"How about you? You get to the heart of the matter with

Laurie Wilkes and get stomped on?"

"My personal life is…"

"Your personal life is a mess. So instead of taking care of it and moving on, you're wallowing around in it like a hog in a mud hole. And behaving like you don't give a damn. But you're making those who *do* give a damn about you crazy with worry. You get your leg or arm, or your neck broken with your act right now, what do you think that would do to Tori? To any of us? Do you think it would make Laurie or her son feel bad and you feel better?"

"That's a ridiculous thing to say."

"Then stop *being* ridiculous. Man up. Get things settled with Laurie once and for all or move on. Then get back to business and act like a champion should act…ride like one. Or are you afraid for some reason?"

Trey felt the anger rise inside him. But then he also felt other emotions. The biggest fact in all that had just been said, was the simple truth. He knew Truitt was right. He usually was. He might have left Laurie behind him almost six weeks ago, but it had felt more like years. Only the knife was still there in his gut. And no matter what he tried to do to dislodge it, it wouldn't budge. It was the pain and anger he felt at himself for being so weak. Why couldn't he get over the woman? She had pushed him away. Laurie had chosen her life in Dallas for her and her son. She wanted no part of him and his life. Yet, there was still something that kept the door from slamming shut between them. And he knew he wasn't proud of the way he had been behaving. Truitt was right. He had become someone he didn't like very much.

"She'll probably slam the door in my face."

Truitt shook his head. "Maybe. But what if she doesn't? You prepared to decide what's more important to you?"

Could there be a chance that Laurie might be glad to see him? The emails that he and T.J. passed back and forth now and then always just mentioned that she was busy. Busy teaching and taking care of the two of them. T.J. missed him. That was the twist of the knife in another way. He missed the little boy. And he missed Laurie more each day instead of less. Truitt was right. He had to face things once and for all.

"How did you get through this pain? You lost one love when she died. And then you almost lost Annie. How did you do it?"

Truitt was silent for a few long moments. "There's nothing worth having more than the person you love returning that love. It makes the world worth living in. And that's why you won't give up, and you'll fight for it with every breath you have. At least that's the way it was for me. And I thank God every day for Annie. I took a chance on loving the second time in my life and what if I hadn't?"

Trey knew what he had to do. Once again his brother had stepped up and given him a swift kick. "You're headed back to Texas tomorrow. You got room on that plane for another cowboy?"

IT HAD BEEN a long day. The end of a long week. Just as all the other six had been before the present week that was about to end. But who was counting? Laurie was looking at an evening ahead that was a little different from the usual Friday. T.J. had left right after school with the rest of his scout group on a trip to a scout camp in the Hill Country. For the first time since they had returned from their summer in McKenna Springs, he had actually shown a bit of excitement at the prospect. Maybe they were beginning to turn a corner, she had thought as she had helped him pack.

But as she parked her car and then walked toward the front door of their first-floor apartment, she realized the silence of being alone wasn't something she relished. It was in the quiet times, the long nights lying awake staring at the ceiling over her bed, when her brain would allow the memories to flood back in of a tall cowboy with the sky-blue eyes and easy smile who could take her breath away with one look, one kiss. And then reality would crash in and she would be left with nothing but pieces of a heart that she doubted would ever be whole again.

Perhaps she'd find a movie to take in, an early evening showing, before the couples on their dates would show up for later times. Or maybe she'd just order some Chinese takeout and binge watch old movies on the television. Her mind took a moment to move from her decisions for the evening ahead and the fact there was a man sitting on the front steps, a large bouquet of yellow roses held in his lap. There was a familiar cowboy hat, and then her heart began to beat wildly inside her chest. Surely, she was just projecting one of her dreams into the moment. But then the man stood up and there was the too familiar and too dear smile.

"Hello." Trey spoke first.

"Hello." Nothing too original. But she was lucky to find her voice for that one word.

"I was afraid I might have the wrong address."

"I was late getting out of school."

"I hope I didn't come at a bad time. You don't have any plans or anything, do you?"

"No…not really. T.J. has gone camping with his scout group so…"

"That's right. I recall him saying something about camping in his email last week. I didn't realize it was this weekend. I'm sorry to miss seeing him."

Was he feeling as awkward as she was?

"I'm sorry. I've forgotten my manners. Would you like to come in?" She stepped on the porch, taking her keys from her purse.

"I suppose I should have called before I just landed on your doorstep uninvited."

The key went into the lock, and she opened the door. Stepping inside she did a quick survey of the living room area with its furnishings in creams and turquoise…nothing fancy, yet she had made it as nice a home for her and her son as she could. Thankfully, she had straightened it up last night when she couldn't go to sleep right away. Setting her purse and book bag on a nearby counter, she turned to the man standing in the middle of the room, his gaze taking in his surroundings.

"Is there a rodeo in town? I haven't heard T.J. mention anything about it."

"These are for you," he said, holding the bouquet that had to be at least two dozen in number with delicate sprigs of baby's breath added throughout the long stems.

Laurie took them and breathed in the heady scent. "They're very beautiful. I do love yellow roses. Thank you." She stood, holding them in her arms.

"If you don't have any plans for this evening, I hope you might agree to have dinner with me."

"I don't have any plans. Dinner would be nice." Why had she agreed? The moment she had said the words, she wished she could take them back. Was she crazy? Spending time with Trey would only make getting over him even more difficult.

"We could leave now, if you're ready."

He wasn't giving her any time to change her mind.

"Let me put these in water and then freshen up a bit. I won't be long. Please have a seat."

She left him and finally breathed a sigh of release of tension once she had escaped to the kitchen. Laurie found a vase under the sink and once she had arranged the flowers in it and filled it with water, she set them in the center of the small dining table in the alcove for the time being. She then hurried down the hall and into her bedroom. What was he doing in Dallas? Why had he come here with flowers in hand? The questions filled her brain as she hastily went through her closet. The navy and white pantsuit she had worn for school that day didn't seem nice enough for dinner.

Trey had appeared on her doorstep dressed in a two-piece dark gray suit, with a white shirt, black boots, and a gray Stetson. He looked every bit the wealthy cowboy rancher come to the big city. She chose a sleeveless deep fuchsia A-line dress with a hint of black lace trim at the bottom hemline that fell just above the knees. It had a matching shawl wrap in the black lace of the hem. Black high heels completed the outfit. She freshened her makeup and dabbed on her best perfume at pulse points. Her hair had been French braided earlier that day and she looked good. She didn't know why she should be so nervous. It was dinner. Nothing else to be read into it.

She found him seated in the living room looking at ease and as if he belonged there. Maybe in her dreams that was how she had imagined it. Laurie needed to remember that this was a reality that wouldn't have him as a permanent resident. He was simply passing through for whatever reason. He had seemed a bit disappointed when he learned T.J. was not home. That was probably why he had really stopped by.

She knew he and her son had kept in touch once or twice a week via short emails. She hadn't minded. It made T.J. happy. And she expected it would wane before too long, as time passed. It was dinner and it would be short and then he'd leave. He stood when he saw her standing in the hallway entrance. His eyes told her that he liked what he saw.

"Sorry if I was a bit longer than first thought."

"No problem. It was worth a few extra minutes. Shall we go?"

He led her to the parking lot where a black luxury sedan waited. She paused for just a moment.

Trey smiled. "They didn't have any pickups available at the airport."

"That explains it." She returned the smile. They both seemed to relax a bit.

He opened the door and she slid into the passenger seat. They headed toward downtown Dallas. She was surprised when he pulled into the drive of one of Dallas's upscale restaurants. A valet opened her door. Then they were inside an elevator and going to the top floor where she stepped out into a glass-enclosed restaurant with views of Dallas and miles beyond. White linen and candlelight and plush carpeting that muted footsteps made her very glad she had taken the time to change into something nicer than a pantsuit. She still felt a bit underdressed though in comparison to some of the other female patrons. Trey on the other hand was clearly treated as a celebrity in their midst. He paid no attention to it. He was focused on making her feel at ease.

Laurie had been a basket of nerves since she arrived home and found Trey on her doorstep. Now, she sat across from him at a table next to the floor-to-ceiling windows with the city displayed below them. It would be heartbreakingly romantic if their history didn't belie the fact. But it seemed Trey was intent on keeping the conversation light and moving along throughout the meal. Maybe they were just a couple of former friends meeting over a shared meal and catching up? One part of her brain said so, while something else kept warning her to keep her guard in place…around her heart. The conversation was on neutral topics, catching up with the latest news in Faris and McKenna Springs. Bringing her up to date on his family. And sharing some amusing anecdotes about his time on the circuit. Trey also drew her out about her and T.J.'s lives since their return to Dallas. She found herself sharing bits and pieces of life in her classroom, and he seemed to really be interested. Before she realized it, they were past the main course and the decision for a dessert was at hand.

"I don't know about you, but I think dessert doesn't interest me tonight. But you please choose something. I'll just have a cup of coffee and watch."

Laurie shook her head. "I'm too full. I think I agree with the no dessert option."

Trey nodded. Then he stood, not bothering to order his coffee. "Let's take a walk."

A beautiful park with flowering gardens and sculptures had been built along the man-made river that flowed around the tall building and around others in the vicinity. The subdued lighting made it a popular location for people living in the high-rise apartment buildings and hotel guests to enjoy the walking trails and benches. There was a light breeze, and Laurie was glad of the shawl as she wrapped it around her shoulders. It provided a bit of warmth from the night air, but it also gave her hands something to do when those nerves began to surface again as they walked.

Trey had fallen silent on the first part of the walk, leaving a somewhat companionable silence to fall over them. Laurie wished she could shake the feeling there was more to his visit. Finally, she could not stay silent. "You never told me what you're doing here. I don't think there's a rodeo in town…is there? And you should be very busy on the circuit right now. I think I heard mention of that fact when T.J. found one of the rodeos on television a couple of weeks back. He was excited to find you riding in it."

That caused Trey to pause and he gave her a long look. "Did you watch?"

"I was grading papers at the dining room table. The television was in the background. Every now and then I took a look at the screen, but mostly I just heard the announcers in the background."

"I see. Guess I was hoping you'd be more interested. Chalk it up to a hit to my over-blown ego." He tried to play it off. Was he disappointed in her response? Why would that matter to him?

"You haven't answered my question, Trey. What brought you to my doorstep today? Were you hoping to stop in and see T.J.? If you had called, I could have saved you a trip."

His attention was full on her. And he stood a lot closer than was helpful to her sanity. But it was time to get some reality infused into the moonlight and flowers. "I didn't come to see T.J. Although I admit I've missed the little guy. And I do thank you for allowing us to exchange emails now and then. As for calling... Well, the number of times I sat and looked at your number on my cell phone, my finger hovering back and forth over it, well that would be in the double digits at least. But I always opted out at the last minute. I didn't think a call from me would exactly be welcome."

That surprised her. "Why would you think that?"

"We didn't exactly part in what I considered the best of friends. In fact, we weren't really friends. I felt you pretty much said you had no interest in any type of future with a rodeo cowboy. There wasn't any stability there and you decided to move on. Was that not your intention the last evening we were together?"

"Why would that matter now? You went back to your life on the circuit, and I came back to my life here as a teacher."

"Well, I went back to the circuit. But not with a clear mind. And as my wise brother Truitt and sister Tori finally got through my hard head, I was headed for another really hard fall if I didn't find some answers and soon. So here I am."

"You said another hard fall... Were you hurt when you went back to the rodeo?" Why hadn't someone told her? Why hadn't T.J. mentioned it? Surely it had been reported on one of those live rodeo programs he watched on cable.

"Would that have mattered to you?" And that question went straight to the heart of it.

Chapter Nineteen

I T WAS APPARENT that his spontaneous question in return to hers had almost stunned her into an abrupt silence. Yet he wasn't sorry he asked it. Maybe it sounded a bit harsh? But it was part of the reason that had brought him a thousand miles to stand in front of her and lay his cards on the table...for everyone's sakes.

"Of course, it would have mattered. I would never wish harm on you. How could you even think that a possibility?"

"I thought we had something between us," he replied. No more games, no more talking around the subject. "I showed more of myself and my world to you than I ever had before...to anyone. Even members of my own family. So I guess I was blindsided how you could just toss it to the side and walk away without a backward glance. I couldn't do that so easily. I became someone I haven't liked very much...nor have those around me. I guess I need to know what happened? Did you ever care, or did I just imagine that part of our relationship?"

"Ever care? Are you crazy? Of course I did...do...whatever. What does that matter now? Our worlds are simply way too different."

Trey felt a sliver of hope for the first time since arriving on her doorstep. His abrupt question had caught her off-guard, and she had replied without thinking it to death or throwing up a smoke screen as to how she really felt.

"I don't see that our worlds are that different. And in the ways they are, that should be where a couple talks about it and comes up with a way to either change things or find a new way of doing things...*together*. My dad was a cowboy in a long line of cowboys when he met my mom. He had inherited a lot of land from his ancestors, and it about killed him to keep it going and build on it over the years. My mom worked as a waitress in the café where her dad was the cook, and her mom was a seamstress and receptionist for the local dentist. But none of that mattered when they met. It took them all of two weeks to decide that their future was together, and they eloped. They never regretted it for one moment. They raised us all in a home filled with unconditional love and laughter. Until the day we lost them. But we all knew that was what we wanted when each of us grew up.

"I'm a rodeo cowboy. I also am a rancher and will go back to that sooner rather than later. And you know my plans for a rodeo school, in addition to punching cows. I want to build a home on the ranch, find my soul mate like Dad did, and have a few little cowboys and cowgirls to bring back the love and laughter I grew up with. I don't think that makes you and me that much different. So what else do you have against me?"

"You're a guy on a poster on my son's wall. You're a celebrity. What do I know about being in that atmosphere? I'm a single mom and a schoolteacher. Half the time I don't know if I even know how to be a good mom. But I'm trying. And I know how important your dream of rodeo has always been to you. I watched you in school…and I saw how you went after it. When T.J. and I came to Dallas this past summer and saw you in your element, it seemed all the more foreign to what we were used to. I guess I thought it was easier to step back and make the inevitable break sooner and not later. The longer it went on, the more T.J. would be hurt when it was over."

Trey wasn't going to let it go that easy.

"Only T.J.? What about you? Were you ready to walk away because it might be easier?"

Laurie went to turn away, but his hand on her arm stopped her. At least she didn't jerk it away from him. And when he allowed his hand to slowly slide down and close around hers, it remained in his grasp. Along with it came a deep sigh from the woman who met his gaze with her own. Was he imagining the shimmer of moisture in the dark blue-green depths?

"None of it was made easier. T.J.'s heart was just as broken. And yes, I missed you, too."

"A little or a lot…how much you missed me?"

Those same eyes sparked back at him. "You want a

pound of flesh or something? Is your ego in that bad of a shape? Okay...*yes*, I missed you a *lot*. I didn't want to. But I did. Satisfied?"

"No, I'm not looking for some sort of payback or whatever. And it doesn't make me satisfied to know that you were unhappy or T.J., either. Because when the two people who've become the most important people in your life push you away and you are too stupid to stand your ground in that moment, then that drives you a little...make that a *lot* of crazy. So much so that you finally get on a plane and end up on a doorstep hiding behind a bunch of flowers, waiting to have them thrown in your face and be told to get lost. And that's why I am in Dallas. There's no rodeo. There's no ranch business. There's just *me*...needing to ask the woman who has my heart if she wants to keep it or not." And there it was. He had no more words. It was up to Laurie who was looking a little shell-shocked after his full confession.

"I have your heart?"

He felt a strange sensation beginning to start around the center of his chest where his heart had been in isolation. "I think that's what I just said. You've had it basically since you attacked me the first time I walked into the store and landed on top of me. You made quite an impression. And I hear that words are important... At least that's what Tori yelled at me as I left for the airport this morning. So here it is. I love you, Laurie Lou Wilkes. I never thought I'd be saying that to anyone in my lifetime. But I hadn't counted on finding you...again. You and T.J. showed me what real life was meant to be. And I knew it was a done deal when I stood in the center of the arena in Denver, and I had just won another saddle and more points toward Vegas. And I couldn't have cared less. The two people I wanted to be with in that moment weren't there. I knew it was time to come here...that and Truitt giving me a few choice words that amounted to a kick in the butt. How about it, Laurie? I'm a cowboy asking a schoolteacher to give him a chance to make her happy for the next few decades or so."

The tears weren't contained any longer. He saw them and his fingers went to catch them and brush them away from her cheeks. "Don't cry. Is it that horrible a proposal?"

She managed to shake her head. "Not horrible. It was probably the most perfect proposal in the whole world of proposals."

"So how about an answer?"

"Yes...yes...yes!" She would have said it louder and several more times, but he had captured her face between his palms and his mouth was covering hers with a delicious soul-bending, mind-numbing kiss. Whether it was several hours or minutes...neither of them made any move to end that kiss.

Until Trey seemed to have remembered something...and he lifted away from her, his hand going to his inside pocket. "I really did have this planned to be more perfect for you...if I was lucky enough to get this far this evening." He stepped back and went down on one knee. Laurie's look was a combination of shock and surprise and so many emotions. Opening his palm, the ring that he had once before used to place on her finger when they thought they might have to fight Chloe for T.J. lay there.

"The diamond band was my mother's. Then my dad wanted to add something she never had when they got married and that was an engagement ring. So he searched for the most beautiful stone he could find and added the emerald-cut diamond on top. It sparkles a lot. Because he said she was the guiding light of the whole family and shone brighter than any star above. I'm sure he made it sound better than I just did. She never saw it though… It was to be her Christmas present, but they died in September. But that's how I feel already about you. If you think it isn't right for you or you want to pick out…."

Laurie's hand closed over his palm and she shook her head. "I fell in love with this ring the moment I saw it that day in the courthouse. And the fact that it blends both the past and a new hope for the future…makes it all the more special to me and I would be proud to wear it. I would feel very connected to your family."

Trey stood and slid the ring onto her ring finger. "This time it's there to stay." And that would be the most heartfelt of all vows to come.

T.J. CAME BOUNDING up the steps and into the apartment. "Mom! It was great! We found a horned toad and...." He stopped abruptly when he saw the tall figure standing behind his mom, his hands on her shoulders.

"Trey! You're here! This is awesome!" And he dropped his backpack as he went straight to wrap his arms around Trey's waist. Laurie's heart, which she thought couldn't get any closer to bursting with happiness, stood to melt as she watched the look cross Trey's face as he folded his arms around the boy's shoulders and returned the hug. Her mother's heart knew pure joy knowing that her son was about to gain a good man for a stepfather...actually the only father figure he had ever known in his life. And one that he already loved and admired.

"It's good to see my best fishing buddy," Trey said. T.J. stepped back, a broad grin splitting his face from ear to ear.

"Can we go fishing while you're here? Can you stay for dinner?"

"Whoa, hold on a minute." The man laughed at the rapid-fire questions. "I'm afraid I have a plane to catch soon so we'll have to take a rain check on the fishing. But I do have time for dinner with you and your mom before I go to the airport. And while your mom is finishing up the meal, I thought you and I might take a walk...catch up on some things. Sound good?"

"That's cool. Is that okay, Mom?" T.J. shot a look over to Laurie. She nodded. "I think that will be good. You two be back in about twenty minutes, okay?"

"I can show you where the basketball court is and the swimming pool, too."

"Lead the way." Trey shot a wink over to Laurie as he turned to follow the excited boy from the apartment. She sent him a grin in return.

"I'm really glad you came to visit. I was afraid you might forget us." T.J. made the statement as they walked across the parking lot toward the common area of the apartment grounds.

Trey shook his head, his steps shortening to allow the boy to walk beside him. "That would not be possible. No way could I ever forget you two. The circuit has kept me pretty busy."

"I know. I saw you ride a couple of times when the rodeos were on the cable channel we get. You were awesome. But I knew you'd win."

Trey smiled. "I'm glad you have such confidence in my ability. I could have used some of that on a couple of those rides. How about we sit a spell over at that picnic table there." Trey nodded to where a table sat under a shade tree in a quiet space of green grass. "There's something important I need to talk over with you."

T.J. nodded and they made their way over and sat down. The boy was very quiet, a solemn look on his face, hands clasped on top of the table in front of him. "Are you going away? And you aren't coming back?"

Trey was surprised by the boy's concerned tone. He shook his head. "I'm going away because I have to get back to the circuit and finish up the season. But I'm coming back and in fact, your mom and I talked it over and you both are going to be there in Vegas at Nationals with me."

Immediately T.J.'s face lit up and the excitement resonated in his voice and body. "That's the championship! We are really going to be there and watch you win?"

He laughed. "Well, you'll be there, but let's not get ahead of ourselves just yet. I'll do my best to win, but there are some very good riders that I've got to beat first."

"I can't wait! I hope the days go really fast."

"I'm glad you're excited about that. And there's something that is really a lot more important that I want to talk to you about. It's pretty serious. And I want you to promise to be very honest with me when I ask you a question in a few minutes. Okay?"

T.J. nodded and sat up straighter. "Okay." He was giving Trey his whole attention and showing his most serious side.

"One of the best days of my life was the day I came into your granddad's store and met you and your mom. And we went fishing and that was fun, too. Even the part where we all went into the water by accident."

T.J. tried to keep his grin from breaking out. Trey smiled.

"We got to know each other. But I had to go away on the rodeo circuit again. Only I realized something very important. I had fallen in love with your mom. And that also included you. So I thought about it a while and then I came here, and I asked your mom to marry me."

The look on the boy's face had definitely frozen in amazement. Trey continued.

"And it is very important that I ask you if you are okay if your mom marries me. Because it involves you, too. I'm asking you and your mom to become a family with me. What do you think? Would that be okay?"

T.J. looked down at his hands that were still clasped on the table. He was giving something deep thought.

"Do you have any questions you need to ask me first?"

"Would…does that mean that you'd be like my dad? And where would we live? Would you move in here?"

Trey appreciated the boy wanted to lay the subject on the table.

"I wouldn't move in here. Once your mom and I got married, you and your mom would come live on the ranch. You'd go to school in Faris, along with Andy and Jamie. And yes, I would be your stepdad. I know you had a birth father. And from what I know of him, he was a very good man who loved you very much and made sure he found the perfect mom for you. I would never think about taking his place."

"Mom tells me stories about my dad. And he left me a video and I saw him and heard his voice and all. What would I get to call you?"

"That is up to you."

"I'll think about it. And my mom? Does she want to marry you?"

"Yes, I believe she does. And I can give you my word, T.J. I will do everything in my power to make your mom and you both happy. I'll always be there for you. What do you think about all of this?"

The boy trained his green gaze on him. "My mom deserves a lot because she works hard, and she always takes care of me. I think someone needs to take care of her some, too. I think you would do that."

"I give you my word on that."

"And it would be really good to have a dad...you know...like the other kids and all. You could teach me some things. Mom tries but she isn't a guy you know? And we could talk about things like guys do."

"We can talk about anything, at any time. I would be very proud to have you as my son...and my fishing buddy."

For a moment, T.J.'s mask slipped and the young boy seeking a dad and a good person to care for his mom shown through. But then, he remembered something, and he squared his shoulders. Standing up, he solemnly extended his hand toward Trey. Trey stood also. They shook hands. "I think it's a good idea. We should be a family."

"That's the best idea anyone has ever had. Let's go tell your mom."

Epilogue

"WELL, GUESS YOU'LL be next." If Tori heard those words one more time that day, she would lose it on that person. That's why she tried to stay away from most people. She grabbed a slice of wedding cake and beat a retreat down the long hallway of the foyer outside the reception area. She pushed open a door and was outside where she made her way down a sidewalk, keeping well away from the merry makers on the terraces overlooking the gardens or dancing in the warmer confines of the ballroom. Tori lifted the skirt of her long burgundy velvet bridesmaid outfit, and then took a seat on one of the benches tucked away behind a bank of greenery. The cake was a delicious Italian crème confection and she relished each bite.

"I thought that was you skulking away from the reception."

"I don't skulk. And don't you think the groom might be missed?" She took another bite of cake as Trey settled himself on the bench next to her.

"What *are* you doing out here and not beside your beautiful bride?"

"She *is* a beautiful bride, isn't she? The most beautiful one I've ever seen."

Tori looked at her brother and the way he said the words and the look on his face, made her shake her head. He had certainly been bitten by the love bug or whatever one might call it. She had seen that look on the faces of her other two brothers when they had wed their wives.

"I also hope you aren't taking your second-place finish at Nationals too much to heart. That Brubek bull did deserve a high number, but I thought it might be too close to call between him and your boy. But as we always say…there's the road to next year ahead of you."

"I've dealt with the disappointment. And you are right. Next year will indeed be ours."

"That's the sister I know." He grinned. "I also came here to give you this. Don't say I never pay a debt." He handed her three crisp fifty-dollar bills. "Go on, take it. You are indeed the…"

"Don't say it." She took the bills in hand. "If I've heard it once, I've heard it fifty times tonight. *You're next. The last one left.* It's like you're headed to an execution or something and people just sound so gleeful about it."

Trey threw his head back and laughed out loud. "Oh my, little sister. You have no idea how wrong we were about the whole matrimonial thing all this time."

"Wrong?"

"When we would sit together after a wedding and place our bets about who would be the next one headed down the aisle…and who would bite the dust last. And what was all the fuss about."

"I prefer being known as the *last smart one standing*. The other sounds a bit morbid."

He slowly shook his head, then stood. "Well, one fine day, I do know for certain…I will get to have the true last laugh when you come walking down that aisle. Because you can run but you can't hide from that slippery cupid and his arrow." Then he raised his gaze and his voice. "Isn't that right, Gray?"

Tori saw the familiar form of the sheriff move down the sidewalk to join them.

"I'm afraid to agree since I only heard a bit of that…something about running and hiding?"

"I'll leave it to my sister to share what you missed…or not. I need to claim another dance with my wife." Then a wide grin split his face. And he had that look in his eyes that Tori had seen earlier. "That does have a nice ring to it, doesn't it?" He left them alone and took the steps to the terrace two at a time.

Gray took his unoccupied seat next to Tori. "I thought you might like these." He reached into his suit jacket and came out with a small bag of lemon candy. He had chosen her favorite candies from the dessert bar in the dining room and brought them to her. Typical Gray. She gave him a smile as she set the empty plate beside the bench and took the candy in hand.

"Thank you. That was thoughtful of you."

His gaze landed on the rolled bills in her one hand. "Is there a card game around here I don't know about?"

Tori shook her head. "Trey owed me for a bet we had. He was paying up. At each wedding, we made a bet about who would be the last Tremayne standing. And that's me. So I won."

Gray nodded but remained quiet. In fact, she had noticed that the last two times she had been back in Faris from the rodeo circuit, he had seemed quieter than usual. She just chalked it up to being busy. She looked at him with eyebrows raised.

He enlightened her with his thoughts. "Maybe it was your brothers that really won. That's the way I might look at it."

Tori was caught off guard. Where was the Gray who was usually sharing a joke or a laugh with her? He looked at her and she felt like he was searching for something.

"But I think you and I just see things in different ways. I guess I might have just realized that recently. Well," he said, standing up, "don't go spending your winnings there all in one place. You don't have any more weddings to bet on." Then he gave her an odd smile and walked back the way he came from and soon was out of her sight.

A minute or so later, a door closed with a loud thud. And she had the most unsettling feeling that it mirrored the sudden feeling that squeezed her insides as she had watched Gray leave.

★

LAURIE SLIPPED OUT onto the balcony of the suite of the hotel where family and friends had been booked for the wedding festivities. She needed a moment. The wedding had been her dream come true. Trey had made certain of that. Their vows had been said in the small community chapel set in beautiful gardens where she and T.J. had been attending services since he was a newborn. Trey had been in total agreement with anything she wanted. He said the only thing that mattered to him was the moment the pastor would declare them husband and wife…and son. He had requested that be added to the vows, and Laurie's heart expanded even more with love for the man.

And last week, they had all been in Vegas at the National Finals. No one yelled louder or longer than T.J. when he watched the man he had decided to call Dad win that World Champion belt buckle.

She looked at the skyline of the city before her. The sun was setting in the west and the golden glare shown off the tall glass-filled walls of the skyscrapers. Christmas was coming next week. Never would she have imagined that six months ago, she would be standing in such a place, dressed in a gorgeous cream satin-and-lace wedding gown with its matching cape, the veil gently drifting around her in the breeze of the early winter's day.

So much had changed for her the day Jonathan Monroe had knocked on her door and asked for her help. He was afraid to die and leave his little son alone in the world. And what if she hadn't said yes that she would take care of little T.J.? So much might have been different. But she had and the road had led her and her little boy on quite a journey. And now she needed to do one more thing before she closed the door on their old life and began the new chapter.

Somewhere between the setting sun and the oncoming stars, there was a place where she hoped Jonathan had found a spot to rest in peace. Laurie closed her eyes and said a prayer for him as she often did throughout the years. But tonight, she had to send her heartfelt thanks. Because of one man's selflessness, another man had asked her and T.J. to begin a family with him. It would be quite an adventure if she knew Trey Tremayne. T.J. would grow tall and strong and have a good father to emulate and allow him to grow into a man that Jonathan would be proud of. She would make a home for them and continue her teaching with Trey cheering her on. And one day, they might be blessed with more children to love and watch grow. The future was theirs.

A smile crossed her lips and a soft whisper escaped them. "Thank you, dear friend. Rest easy now. We're home."

The End

Don't miss the final book in the Tremaynes of Texas…
The Sheriff and the Cowgirl.
Coming September 2021, pre-order now!

Join Tule Publishing's newsletter for more great reads and weekly deals!

If you enjoyed *The Bronc Rider Takes a Fall,*
you'll love the next book in….

The Tremaynes of Texas series

Book 1: *Capturing the Texas Rancher's Heart*

Book 2: *The Rancher Risks It All*

Book 3: *The Bronc Rider Takes a Fall*

Book 4: *The Sheriff and the Cowgirl*
Coming September 2021!

Available now at your favorite online retailer!

More books by Debra Holt

The Blood Brothers series

Book 1: *True Blue Cowboy*

Book 2: *Homeward Bound, Cowboy*

Book 3: *Her Secret Cowboy*

The Texas Lawmen series

Book 1: *Beware the Ranger*

Book 2: *The Lawman's Apache Moon*

Book 3: *Along Came a Ranger*

Book 4: *The Sheriff's Christmas Angels*

Available now at your favorite online retailer!

About the Author

Born and raised in the Lone Star state of Texas, Debra grew up among horses, cowboys, wide open spaces, and real Texas Rangers. Pride in her state and ancestry knows no bounds and it is these heroes and heroines she loves to write about the most. She also draws upon a variety of life experiences including working with abused children, caring for baby animals at a major zoo, and planning high-end weddings (ah, romance!).

Debra's real pride and joys, however, are her son, an aspiring film actor, and a daughter with aspirations to join the Federal Bureau of Investigation (more story ideas!). When she isn't busy writing about tall Texans and feisty heroines, she can be found cheering on her Texas Tech Red Raiders, or heading off on another cruise adventure. She read her first romance, Janet Dailey's *Fiesta San Antonio*, over thirty years ago and became hooked on the genre. Writing contemporary western romance is both her passion and dream come true, and she hopes her books will bring smiles…and sighs…to all who believe in happily-ever-after's.

Thank you for reading

The Bronc Rider Takes a Fall

If you enjoyed this book, you can find more from all our great authors at TulePublishing.com, or from your favorite online retailer.

TULE
PUBLISHING

Made in the USA
Columbia, SC
30 September 2023